Dear Reader,

As you can see, we've taken a little trip out west. I'd like to personally welcome you to Jasper, Montana, home of THE LANDRY BROTHERS.

I can't take total credit for this; my editor, Natashya Wilson, has family in Montana. She was telling me all about the things she did there, and I decided it would be a perfect place to raise seven boys.

Well, they're all grown up now and it's my job to find each one of them the perfect mate. I started at the logical place, with Sam Landry, the oldest of the clan. Sam is a perfect father and a wonderful man, even if he is a bit staid. I sent Callie to lighten him up a little.

Even before the first word is spoken between these two, they have something very, very special in common. This is a story about secrets—some bad and some very good.

Inside, there is a sneak peek at brother Seth's story—*Landry's Law*, available in December 1999. Please watch for the rest of the Landry brothers and let me know what you think. You can always reach me at Harlequin Books, 300 E. 42nd Street, New York, New York, 10017.

Happy Reading!

Kelsey Roberts

Kelsey Roberts
His Only Son

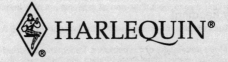

HARLEQUIN®

TORONTO • NEW YORK • LONDON
AMSTERDAM • PARIS • SYDNEY • HAMBURG
STOCKHOLM • ATHENS • TOKYO • MILAN • MADRID
PRAGUE • WARSAW • BUDAPEST • AUCKLAND

To Natashya Wilson,
for her incredible patience,
thanks for helping me through this one.

ISBN 0-373-22535-0

HIS ONLY SON

Copyright © 1999 by Rhonda Harding Pollero

Visit us at www.romance.net

Printed in U.S.A.

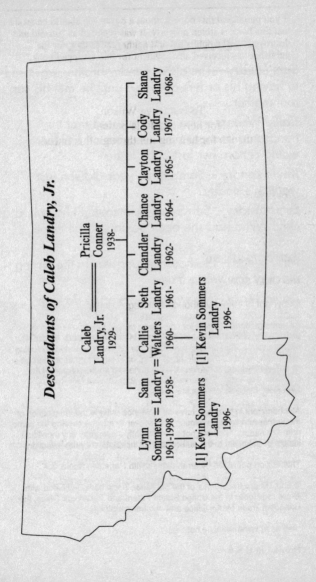

Descendants of Caleb Landry, Jr.

Caleb
Landry, Jr. ═══ Pricilla
1929-   Conner
               1938-

Lynn   Sam   Callie   Seth   Chandler   Chance   Clayton   Cody   Shane
Sommers = Landry = Walters   Landry   Landry   Landry   Landry   Landry   Landry   Landry
1961-1998   1958- 1960-   1961-   1962-   1964-   1965-   1967-   1968-

[1] Kevin Sommers   [1] Kevin Sommers
    Landry   Landry
    1996-   1996-

CAST OF CHARACTERS

Sam Landry — The oldest Landry brother was used to having his orders obeyed — until he met his son's real mother.

Callie Walters — She never guessed that the handsome stranger sweeping her off her feet would restore her lost baby to her.

Kevin Landry — Sam's three-year-old son just wants his daddy.

Lynn Landry — Sam's late wife couldn't have had a child. Who had she been paying off all those years?

Mrs. Lange — The housekeeper was in the wrong place at the wrong time.

David Leary — He wanted nothing to do with Callie and her child — or so he said.

Brittany Johnson Leary — She had more reason than anyone to resent Callie.

Taylor Reese — Was the new housekeeper too good to be true?

Mason Walters — Callie's father had disowned his pregnant daughter.

Mary Walters — Callie's stepmother helped all she could — but whom was she really helping?

Jim York — The P.I. suddenly disappeared.

Prologue

"I got here as soon as I could," Sam said. "What's the big emergency?"

Miles Johnson was wearing his lawyer face. That blank, unreadable expression he donned during negotiations. "Have a seat."

Sam didn't feel like sitting. Instead, he braced his hands on the back of the leather chair opposite Miles's mahogany desk. He checked his watch. "I've got to pick Kevin up from the sitter in twenty minutes. If this is about the Littlefield merger, I've—"

"It's about Kevin," Miles said in a soft, even tone.

Sam's heart skipped. He had feared this moment since the death of his wife eight months earlier. Four of his six brothers had warned him, tried to prepare him for this possibility.

Sam stepped forward and fell into the chair. "You found him? Kevin's biological father wants him back?"

Miles shook his head. "No. The investigator I hired couldn't find anything listed on the birth certificate you provided."

Rubbing the late-day stubble on his chin, Sam tried to decide if that was good news or bad. Bad, probably. Part of him was glad the guy was nowhere to be found. Still, he knew he needed to find Kevin's birth father to get the waiver. According to Miles, it was the best way to proceed with the adoption.

"So now we do the posting, right?" Sam asked. "Tell me what the notices have to say, and I'll get them into the newspapers by the end of the week."

Miles cleared his throat as he shuffled some papers on his desk. "There's a problem."

Sam's chest seized. "You found a blood relative? You told me that I could still go for the adoption even if you found someone with a biological link to Kevin. You said the courts would take into consideration the fact that Kevin's lived with me since he was four months old. I'm the only father the kid knows." Sam opened and closed his fists.

"Kevin's finally adjusted to Lynn being gone. I'm not going to sit back and let some stranger with the right DNA yank him away from me."

Miles lifted one hand. "Calm down, Sam. As far as I can tell, Lynn didn't leave behind any living relatives. That much of her personal history has proven true."

"What do you mean, 'that much'?"

Miles slid a piece of paper across the desk. "Lynn was born in Ohio. Her father was killed during a military training exercise before her birth. Her mother died of complications from influenza when Lynn was seventeen.''

''I know all that.'' Sam sighed as he briefly scanned the report from the investigator. ''The courts emancipated her instead of putting her into the system.''

Miles shook his head. ''Not according to Child Services in Ohio. Lynn was placed with a family in Canton.''

''Canton?'' Sam repeated, surprised that it didn't bother him more to discover that his late wife may have lied. ''Okay, so she had a foster family. You aren't suggesting that they have a legitimate claim for Kevin? Forget it.''

''Nothing like that,'' Miles assured him. ''But they did provide some interesting information. Sam, it isn't good.''

He took in a deep breath, held it, then exhaled slowly. ''So tell me.''

''Do you know what endometriosis is?''

Sam shrugged. ''Some sort of female thing.''

Miles nodded. ''It's a condition that causes painful scarring internally.''

''She wasn't in pain when we were married,'' Sam said. ''So what does this have to do with Kevin?''

''Because of her condition, Lynn had to have surgery when she was with the foster family.''

''She had a scar,'' Sam remembered. ''She said it was from an appendectomy.''

''It was from an emergency hysterectomy.''

Sam laughed without humor. "How can that be possible? She didn't have Kevin until she was thirty-six."

"No, Sam, she didn't have Kevin. She couldn't."

Sam's gut knotted as he leveled his gaze on his attorney. "There has to be a mistake."

"I verified this information with the hospital where the surgery was done. Lynn had a complete hysterectomy just before her eighteenth birthday."

"So what are you telling me?" Sam demanded.

"Lynn could not have given birth to Kevin."

Sam blinked as his mind raced. "Then who did?"

Chapter One

"There is a God," Callie Walters sighed. She looked out at the man climbing out of the sleek car parked in front of her home and studio. Normally she didn't notice cars or men. The only male she was interested in was Michael. She didn't want anything to distract her from her search. However, in this case *normally* didn't apply to the car or the man.

The Jaguar was a shiny champagne convertible—impressive and classy. It paled badly in comparison to its driver. Callie's heart stopped as she admired more than six feet of masculine perfection. Her artist's eyes saw the beauty in his fluid motions, saw the perfect symmetry of his dark, chiseled features. In short, the guy was perfect.

"He's probably gay," she sighed. Callie brushed a few strands of hair off her forehead and smoothed the front of her denim work shirt. "Let him be gay," she added when she did a quick mental comparison. He had on a custom-tailored suit she guessed was as Italian as his soft leather loafers. She was wearing a baggy pair of chinos, one of her father's old T-shirts, the overshirt—also her father's cast-off—and a pair of tennis shoes so worn that her little toes peeked out.

Taking a deep breath, she reached for the doorknob and forced herself to wait for his knock. She couldn't stop herself from feeling that fleeting rush of anticipation. Even after all this time, she still held on to the hope that someday the miracle would happen. Someday her prayers would be answered. Was this gorgeous creature going to tell her what she had longed to hear for three long years?

"Miss Walters?"

Incredible voice. Deep, like the tiny lines on either side of his eyes. Eyes that resembled rich, dark chocolate. She smiled brightly. "That's me."

He seemed tense and a little awkward as well as too handsome to be real. "I'm Sam Landry."

The name was vaguely familiar. Tilting her head back, she met his gaze. "Of the Jasper Landrys?"

He relaxed. He smiled. She melted. "Guilty," he answered. Callie took a step back and motioned for him to come inside. He seemed to fill her studio. It wasn't just the fact that he was tall and broad-shouldered. It had more to do with his presence. Sam Landry didn't enter a room, he dominated it.

Callie moved and cleared a pile of open art books off one of the mismatched chairs in the living room-studio. Depositing them on the floor with a loud thump, she grinned and said, "Have a seat and tell me why one of the infamous Landry brothers has come calling.''

He didn't take the chair. Instead, he walked to the painting on her easel. Quietly he looked at the painting while he absently stroked the faint stubble on his chin. ''The cabin out by Brock's Pass, right?''

She was flattered and flustered all at once. Flattered that he would recognize the setting, considering how little of the painting was finished. Flustered by the way her body was tuned to the scent of his cologne. A woodsy scent that managed to be masculine and subtle all at once. She hadn't had this kind of reaction in years and she found it quite disconcerting.

''Y-yes, it is. It's pretty close to your family's ranch, isn't it?''

He nodded. The action caused some of his thick, ebony hair to fall forward. Automatically he used his square-tipped fingers to rake it back into place. ''I see I came to the right place. Mrs. Tabor over at the Mountainview Inn in Jasper sent me.''

''She's a doll,'' Callie remarked.

''I admired the painting of yours she has hanging behind the counter.''

Callie sighed. ''The Mountainview may not be the Louvre, but it often results in interesting tourists passing through. Are you here to see some completed paintings?'' Instantly she thought about what a sale would mean. She could call Jim York and get him working again. The P.I. had been there less than a minute before Landry drove up. His last lead had taken him to another dead end. He needed more money to continue working. Money she didn't have, which made the prospect of selling a painting important.

"No. I have something else in mind."

Callie nearly burst into tears. Mustering a pleasant smile, she asked, "Such as?"

"Will you take a commission?"

You bet your life. Don't get too excited, she warned herself. *Don't come off as desperate. Even though I am?* A commission could prove to be the answer to her prayers! It would take her one step closer to finding her baby.

Callie had to force herself not to drop to her knees and kiss his feet. Sam Landry had no way of knowing that the simple offer of a commission did make him a god in her eyes.

"What kind of commission?" she asked. "But I have to warn you, I don't paint children."

His dark eyes flashed, then the smile settled back into place. "I want you to paint scenes from the Lucky 7 for my office. I was thinking a group of four? Perhaps depicting the seasons?"

"What size?"

He shrugged. The action caused the olive, raw silk jacket to strain against well-defined muscle. "Twenty-eight by forty? I'll pay whatever your going rates are, of course."

Callie wanted to yell with unbridled glee. "That's a fairly expensive undertaking. You must have a pretty impressive office if you're willing to pay my rates for four paintings, Mr. Landry."

"Sam," he corrected rather stiffly. "I work at Sills, Cartwright and Hingle in Jasper. It was her turn to shrug. "Sorry, is that some kind of law firm?"

"Investment counselors," he supplied.

She smiled, still thinking about how much she could earn on the commission. Maybe enough to finally lead her to Michael. "That's why I'm not familiar with it. I'm not exactly investment material."

"You never know," he said, "I can review your financial status and make some suggestions."

Callie laughed. "My financial status is one step above poverty level, but thank you."

"You've got a lot of talent," he said casually.

It was weird. He would speak, but Callie was having a hard time getting a read on the man. Maybe because he had yet to meet her eyes. Still, she thanked him. "All I need is some gallery owner to think so. Then I'll be able to stop decorating shop windows and painting backgrounds for school plays and church productions."

"Sounds like honest work," Sam said, then he checked his watch. It was one of those chronograph things that cost roughly as much as her modest home. "I've got an appointment here in Helena. I'll be back to take you to dinner this evening so we can agree on terms for the commission." He turned toward the door.

"Wait!" She nearly reached out and grabbed his sleeve. "You don't have to take me to dinner. We can settle this right now."

"I insist," he said as he strode to the door. "I'll pick you up at eight."

Callie was still gaping at his autocratic back as he closed the door. Too bad so much arrogance was wrapped in such a pretty package, she mused.

IT WAS DARK WHEN SAM pulled up in front of Callie's house. Raking his hand through his hair, he hesitated briefly before getting out of the car. Callie Walters wasn't what he had expected. Not at all. He had pictured a broken, miserable shell of a human being, and instead he'd found a beautiful woman who seemed a blend of incredible strength and unbearable pain.

Sam stayed in the car for a moment, parked in the wide driveway of the converted firehouse. He was in dangerous territory. He took in the outline of the old building, nestled among renovated buildings. Apparently Callie had yet to renovate. Somehow the building seemed to suit her, he decided. The dual arched doors once used by horse-drawn fire wagons were now the windows for her first-floor studio. He guessed that had something to do with light. The only real sign that this was now a home was a near-dead potted plant hanging next to the small door in front of his car. Callie might be an artist, but she sure wasn't a gardener.

Through the large, arched windows he could see right into her studio. Watch her paint a few strokes, step back, observe her work and then repeat the process.

Callie Walters was a petite woman with the face of an angel. Even from this distance Sam could see the pain that haunted eyes that were neither blue nor green, but an exotic mix of the two. She had dainty features and a small, perfectly shaped mouth. He was still trying to evaluate her as a potential candidate when she turned and looked directly at him.

He finally got out of the car and went to the door. She opened it and glared up at him. The dim glow of the streetlamp gave her a definite ethereal glow, even if it was a little on the hostile side. Her pale blond hair was cut in a practical bob that just brushed her shoulders. It was her eyes that caused his chest to tighten. They were big and expressive. It was hard to make out her shape, given that she was practically covered by a paint-splattered shirt. Her face was another matter altogether.

"Yes?" she asked rather curtly.

Sam's stomach knotted even more. "We made a dinner appointment?" he reminded her. He tried to keep his nervousness out of his tone. He didn't want her getting suspicious. Not until his mission was complete.

"You made plans," she responded. "I don't take orders well."

"Look," Sam breathed, trying to sound apologetic, "I suppose I could have been more polite, but we both know you need the money, so I didn't think it was necessary to quibble over when and how we came to terms on your commission."

An angry light danced in her eyes. "I can stand right here and tell you my price."

No! his brain screamed. Instantly he offered her his brightest smile. "I'm sure you could. But I'm...I've had meetings all afternoon and I'm really hungry."

"Then go eat."

Sam's gut lurched. "It would be my pleasure if you would join me for dinner."

He watched indecision begin to replace the anger. Then he saw a flash of something else. A raw emotion. The kind that made him instinctively want to reach out and hold her. Sam shoved his hands in his pockets. *Where the hell had that idea come from?*

He realized her anger was an improvement over the haunting pain that he now saw in her eyes. He maintained appropriate decorum, even though his body seemed to be at odds with his intellect. But his intellect wasn't being tempted by her faint, floral perfume.

This was no time to be thinking about perfume. He had a mission that *required* getting her to go with him.

"Since you've asked nicely," Callie said, shrugging off her overshirt and lifting the thin strap of her small purse over her head to settle on one shoulder. "I haven't been out to dinner in a long time."

"I find that hard to believe," Sam remarked. She had dressed in a long skirt and bulky sweater that fell past her hips. He still couldn't make out her shape. All he could tell was that she was small. There was just a hint that Callie was perfectly proportioned. Somehow that hint was sexier than if she'd worn a skin-tight skirt and blouse. One thing was for certain, she was definitely beautiful. He was definitely in trouble.

The last time he had been instantly attracted to a woman, he had ended up in a horrible marriage. Sam would never make that mistake again. *Lord! Why am I thinking about marriage when this woman could potentially ruin my life?*

"Where are we going?" she asked, once she was settled in the passenger seat of his Jag.

"The Mountainview Inn."

"That's an hour away," she remarked.

Sam nearly panicked. "I…um, really like the food there."

She seemed to buy his lame excuse. He wanted to do this on his territory. Besides, he didn't want to risk anyone in Helena linking the two of them. At least, not until he had what he wanted from her.

"Fair enough," she sighed, running her fingertips over the polished-walnut console. "This is pretty impressive."

He shrugged, feeling suddenly pretentious. "It's just a car."

She laughed. It was a deep, breathy sound. This woman exuded sensuality. Bedroom eyes, sultry voice, incredible beauty. The trinity of trouble.

"I drive 'just a car,'" she teased. "This is a sculpted piece of art."

Sam fumbled nervously with the knot of his tie.

"If I'd have known it was going to be an issue, I would have brought my pickup."

He felt her eyes on him. "I have a no-pickup-truck rule."

He couldn't help but laugh. The last thing he'd expected was for her to have a sense of humor. If his research was correct, he wondered how she managed to get through a day. "That's a tall order in Montana. A lot of folks in these parts drive pickups."

"I've never had a good date with a guy in a pickup," she explained. "Not that this is a date, per se," she instantly clarified.

"Right," he agreed quickly. Maybe too quickly. "I mean. This is a business dinner. To discuss a business proposition."

She sighed loudly. "Which is good for my bank account, which apparently you already know is dangerously low."

Sam swallowed and turned to briefly glance at her. "Are you always this...open?"

"My level of poverty isn't exactly a secret here in Helena. Or didn't you notice that I have the only unrestored house on the street?"

Sam's grip tightened on the steering wheel. "Do you have a problem with overspending?"

She made a dismissive little sound. "There's only one thing I overspend on, and trust me, it's worth it."

"It isn't a drug habit or—"

"Geez, Landry. Thanks for thinking so highly of me."

"I don't know you."

"I don't know you, either," she said, breaking the awkward silence. "So, I guess I'll start with the standard questions. Are you gay or married?"

Sam cleared his throat. "I'm not gay."

"Married then?"

He shook his head. "My wife died almost a year ago."

"Enough said." Callie reached out and patted his arm. The feel of her hand on him, even for that brief moment, was electric. So much so that he fairly jumped out of his skin.

"I also have a no-rebound rule, so you're safe." she said, then spent the remainder of the hour-long ride asking him about his work. She seemed genuinely interested when he discussed various investment trends. By the time they arrived at the restaurant, he was even more tense. When this evening was over, he would have what he needed. *Then what?* he wondered. *I'll cross that bridge later,* he swore as he led her inside the wooden A-frame building.

"Evening, Mr. Sam," Belinda, the hostess, greeted. "I've got you a nice table in the back."

It didn't escape Sam's notice that as they wove through the dining room Callie turned heads. For a small woman she had incredible presence.

"Tim will be your waiter," Belinda said as she passed out menus. "You folks enjoy your meal."

Callie was even more beautiful by candlelight. As she studied the menu, he studied her. He couldn't help it. He was looking for some tangible sign, something that would prove or disprove his suspicions.

"I'm not on the menu, Landry," she said without looking up.

"I didn't mean to stare."

She lifted her eyes. They sparkled with amusement. "Liar. I'm not embarrassed to admit that you fall in the gorgeous category. Will that wipe the guilty look from your face?"

Sam couldn't believe it! He was blushing. He knew it, felt the heat on his cheeks. The very last thing he needed was her admission that she found him attractive. This was supposed to be an easy in and out. He couldn't afford any complications. His uneasiness intensified. "You're very blunt."

"Open," she corrected. "You *are* gorgeous. And unless you've never looked in a mirror, you already know that."

Sam smiled through his awkwardness. Luckily Tim arrived to take their drink orders. Callie declined. Sam panicked and insisted. "Some wine? They have an excellent list."

"I'm sure they do," Callie remarked. "I don't drink."

Great! Now what? "I'm sure the bartender can make you something without alcohol."

Tilting her head, she stared at him for a second, confusion in her eyes. "Fine. How about a Virgin Mary?"

Sam felt himself relax, then ordered bourbon for himself. "I don't like to drink alone."

Her expression told him she wasn't buying his explanation, but she let it pass.

"So what do you have in mind for your office?"

"I want paintings of the ranch." He reached into the breast pocket of his jacket. "I brought you these pictures. These are some of my favorite spots on the property."

Callie took the photographs and looked at each one for a long time. When she was finished, she passed them back across the table. "Landscapes shouldn't take me that long. I'll need to go out to the ranch to—"

"Ou-out to my ranch?" he stammered.

Callie tilted her head to one side. "I promise not to poach any of your cattle."

"Are you always this sarcastic with a potential customer?"

"That was a joke, Mr. Landry." She quoted him a price for the work, but he barely made note of it.

"That's fine," he answered.

He saw just a hint of excitement in her eyes, marred only by the whisper of pain still present.

"Thank you. I'll need half up-front and half on completion, fair?"

"Fair."

"Good, I know you're a famous Landry, but I still need to get some of the money up-front. I've found that it's a real motivator to keep people from changing their minds and leaving me stuck." Then she shrugged her delicate shoulders. "By the way, I wasn't being sarcastic before, I was making an attempt at humor. Haven't you ever heard the cliché about laughing being better than crying?''

His chest caught just thinking about what she must have suffered. ''I didn't mean to make it sound like you aren't welcome on the ranch,'' Sam said. ''I just thought you could work from the photographs.''

''I could, but I'd prefer to see the actual places. Is that a problem?''

Huge problem! ''No. I'm sure I can arrange something with Shane.''

''Another one of the Landry brothers?'' she asked.

Tim brought their drinks and took their food orders. It gave Sam an opportunity to regroup. If he continued to act like a jerk, she was bound to get suspicious.

''Shane's the baby,'' he said. ''In every sense of the word.''

Callie laughed as she twirled the celery stalk and the straw in her glass. ''Where are you in the birth order?''

''I'm the oldest.''

She nodded. ''That explains your latent hostility toward your youngest sibling.''

''My hostility is a result of his juvenile behavior,'' Sam announced. ''Shane's idea of solving a problem is to run from it.''

''What's yours?''

Sam started at the question. She was getting dangerously close to personal. ''I guess I try to explore a problem, then weigh possible solutions.''

''The cautious, responsible one, eh?''

"That would more accurately be Cody. He's so cautious he can't commit to anything." He sipped his drink. "Before you ask, Cody is the next to youngest. He's a federal marshal, current whereabouts unknown."

"One of your brothers is the sheriff here, right?"

"Seth. He's next to me. Then there's Chandler."

"Is he the one on TV?" Callie asked.

"WMON's star investigative reporter. Chance is a year younger than Chandler. He's a general practitioner here in Jasper."

"Having a brother who is a doctor is a nice family perk," Callie said. "And the last one?"

"Clayton," Sam said, feeling the stab in his heart. "He was a lawyer."

"I know," she said without any censure. "His trial and conviction were headline news for weeks."

"What about you?" Sam asked.

"I'm an only child," she told him. "My mother died when I was little. My stepmother and I are somewhat close."

"Is your father still alive?"

She shrugged, and he saw a flash of something cloud her expression for a second. "Yes, but we haven't spoken for a little over three years."

"That's tough," Sam remarked, not knowing what else to say, except that he needed to steer her to the subject of her son.

"It's his choice. I had a fall from grace, and my father wasn't able to forgive me."

"That is unfortunate. I have some experience at being abandoned by a parent."

"Really? I'm sorry for you."

Sam felt a pang of guilt. She was being honest and open with him and all he could do was split his attention from her face to her drink and wait for the perfect opportunity.

"My mother chose to leave the family years ago. It was quite difficult on some of my brothers."

"What about you?"

Sam shrugged and lowered his eyes to his glass. "I was already out on my own when she left. I'm sure she'll show up again someday. Just as I'm sure you and your father can work something out. It's inevitable. Most families eventually come to terms."

"You don't know Mason Walters. I didn't, either, I guess. Not the real one."

"I didn't mean to dredge up unpleasant thoughts." *At least, not these unpleasant thoughts. Think, Sam! You need information.*

Callie offered a weak grin. "Stuff happens. The rift with my father isn't the worst thing that's ever happened to me."

"Really?" Sam asked carefully, watching her face intently. He contained his interest by keeping his tone impartial and relaxed.

She tilted her head and met his gaze. "All artists are tortured, Landry. Haven't you ever heard that?"

She was just going to leave it there! He needed to nudge her, so he asked, "What tortures you?"

Her chin thrust out with determination as she

stared at the flickering flame of the candle. "My son was kidnapped. I have to believe that I'll see him again someday."

Sam wasn't sure what to say, so he remained silent.

"Whew," she said on a breath. "I don't know why I'm telling you this."

"I don't mind."

"Sure you do," Callie insisted. "You didn't invite me to dinner to discuss my personal life. Don't worry, Landry. I'm fully functional now. I spent the first year stopping every person with a stroller just to check for Michael. I graduated to talk shows and milk cartons. I have a private detective that searches for him when I have the cash to pay him. Which, by the way, is where I overspend."

"Michael?" Sam repeated.

Callie smiled with a heavy sadness. "Yes. I know he's okay."

"How?"

"Letters."

"From who?"

"The kidnapper."

"What?" Sam fairly barked. "The kidnapper has stayed in contact with you? Do you know him or her?"

Callie shook her head. "Her. Of course not. If I knew her, I'd have my son back."

"You don't have any clues to her identity?"

"No. She's been sending me letters about him since she stole him from the hospital. The FBI thinks she feels guilty, and sending me the letters is her way of easing her guilt.''

"Can't they trace the letters?"

Callie shook her head. "Generic stationery, generic ink. No fingerprints, self-adhesive envelopes and stamps, so no DNA.''

"Where are they from?''

"Different states," Callie explained. "Mostly from Montana, though. So I take comfort in knowing that my son is close and being well cared for.''

"That's incredible. You're a very strong woman, Callie.''

Sam suddenly found himself impressed by her pain and her ability to cope. She was, in short, a remarkable woman.

She shrugged. "Now, maybe. I was pretty devastated for a couple of years. Jim York, my investigator, would get a lead, I'd get all excited, then it wouldn't pan out and I'd hit bottom. Now I don't latch on to every lead. I can't live like that. When I get my son back, I want to be sane.''

He reached across the table and picked up the plastic straw she had discarded. He began bending and twisting it as he considered her situation. "You seem pretty sane to me," Sam insisted. "And very resilient.''

"And very unprofessional," Callie commented. "Let's enjoy dinner. I told you I haven't been out for ages.''

CALLIE COULDN'T REMEMBER the last time she'd had such a relaxing evening. Sam could be as charming as he was handsome, though she sensed he had his guard up and wondered why. She'd stupidly brought up all her emotional baggage, but it hadn't spoiled their meeting. In fact, Sam seemed to have placed her on a pedestal. It was scary, having a man think so highly of her after all this time. Heck, Sam Landry was just scary, period. She was continually reminding herself on the drive home that the guy was in mourning. Rebound relationships were never good. Sam was so wonderful that she considered the possibility of having a casual relationship with him, but that notion was quickly dismissed. She didn't want a relationship with any man until she found Michael.

When he parked in front of her house, Callie fidgeted in her seat. "I'd invite you in for a drink, but I only have bottled water and coffee."

"No problem, it's late. I have to get home, anyway," Sam said. "Some other time."

"Thanks for dinner," she said as she got out of the car. Sam followed. "You don't need to walk me home, Landry. This wasn't a date, remember?"

Her easy smile was erased when she reached the entryway. She recognized the newspaper clipping tacked to the door instantly. Her pulse pounded in her ears, and she started to fall back. Sam's arms were around her just as the strangled cry fell from her lips.

Chapter Two

Seth arrived shortly after the local authorities. He whispered something to the officer in charge before coming to where Sam stood with his arm around Callie's shoulder.

"Miss Walters," he said, tipping the brim of his Stetson.

"Sheriff," she returned in a soft voice.

Sam watched her transform before his very eyes. She went from a state of near terror to a woman almost completely in charge of herself. It was as if she had called upon a well of strength deep within herself. Letting out a long breath, she shrugged out of his hold and ran one unsteady hand through her hair. "I'm sorry Sam called you all the way out here. The sergeant doesn't think there's anything worth investigating."

Sam looked at his brother and asked, "Can't you do something?"

Seth grabbed Sam's sleeve and pulled him aside for privacy. "Want to tell me what this is all about?"

Sam glanced over his shoulder. Once he was certain Callie was occupied by one of the Helena PD officers, he said, "I think this is my fault."

"I gathered that much," Seth drawled.

Sam gave his brother a warning look. Seth seemed to take everything in stride. His brother was normally the first person to point out the obvious. "Did you see the message?"

"'Leave it alone,'" Seth recited from memory. "Does this have something to do with Kevin?"

Sam sucked in a breath and let it out slowly. "I don't know. I just don't like the coincidence. But no one knew I was taking her to dinner. This makes no sense."

"Let's think for a minute," Seth suggested. "If Lynn kidnapped Callie's son three years ago, there's no way she could have left the clipping with the warning unless she rose from the dead to do it."

Sam nodded. "I thought about that already. Obviously Lynn didn't do it, but I still can't rule out the possibility that Kevin is Callie's missing son, Michael."

"Michael, huh? What does she think?" Seth asked.

Sam lowered his voice another notch. "I haven't told her."

"What?" Seth demanded in a harsh whisper. "I know you love the kid. Hell, we all do. But you aren't God, Sam."

Sam took his brother by the arm and led him out onto the front porch. "I just spent the evening listening to her tell me about her missing child. She's been through the wringer. She all but told me that any more false hope would kill her. I'm not going to say anything until I'm sure. She doesn't deserve to be hurt any more than she already has been.''

Seth was shaking his head in blatant disapproval. ''You might have her kid, Sam. You shouldn't keep that from her. Or from the authorities.''

''Just for a little while,'' Sam promised. ''Just until I get the DNA results from the lab.''

''How do you plan on doing that without her knowing?''

Sam reached into his jacket pocket and revealed the tip of the drinking straw he had pilfered during their meal. ''Please send this to the lab first thing in the morning. I've already had Chance swab Kevin's mouth. Once we get the results we'll know for sure. Then, if Kevin is hers, I'll tell her.''

Seth tipped his hat back on his head. ''You're playing with fire, big bro. And I think you're going to get burned.''

''Thanks for the support,'' Sam grumbled. ''I'm going about this the only way I know how. I have to protect Kevin and Callie. I have a responsibility not to act rashly.''

''What about her?'' Seth challenged. ''Why can't you tell her the truth? What about your responsibility to the truth?''

''And destroy her when it turns out Kevin isn't hers?''

"Are you sure you're thinking about her and not yourself?"

Sam pressed his fingers to his temples. "I'm not going to give Kevin up without a fight. Besides, tonight pretty much proves that Kevin isn't her missing son. Lynn turned out to be a witch, but I doubt even she could come back from the dead to taunt Callie."

The team of local cops came outside. "We'll be on our way," the older of the two said. "I'll send this to the FBI agent in charge of the kidnapping case."

His tone told Sam he thought the effort would be a waste of time.

"Could you burn me a copy of that?" Seth asked.

The officer shrugged. "I don't see why not. I'll send it to your office."

"Thanks," Sam said.

The men shook hands, and then Sam and his brother went back inside Callie's house. She gave them a bright but forced smile. "Thanks for staying. And thanks for coming out here," Callie said to Seth. "Would you like a cup of coffee before you drive back?"

Sam was about to say no when Seth quickly responded, "We sure would."

When Callie went into the adjoining room, he turned to his brother and asked, "Why are we hanging around?"

"I want a look at the letters you told me about on the phone. The ones she's been getting from the kidnapper."

''Good idea,'' Sam admitted, sorry he hadn't thought to ask about them himself.

While Callie made coffee, Sam took a closer look at her home. The interior walls were brick, and some faded stenciling was still visible. The huge open space served as her home and studio. A set of circular stairs led to a second-floor loft, which he guessed was her bedroom. He wondered if it was as cluttered and disorganized as the first floor. Everywhere he looked, he found stacks of books, pages torn from magazines, sketches and finished paintings. The chairs, sofa and dining table all appeared to be sec-ondhand and there was no apparent scheme. The For-mica table in the galleylike kitchen area was scarred and chipped, the chairs covered in tattered turquoise vinyl. The sofa was decorated with a woven throw in bright, primary colors. The other chairs were mis-sion-style with worn cane seats.

Amazingly, she had somehow managed to make the eclectic blend work, mostly through the use of her artwork. A dozen or so paintings graced the walls, incorporating many of the colors into a har-monious blend.

Callie brought a pot of coffee and three mugs into the main space. Her tray was a piece of stretched canvas. ''I hope you like hazelnut.''

''Fine,'' both men said in unison.

Seth settled into the closest chair, leaving Sam and Callie to the sofa. When he sat next to her, again he noticed the faint scent of her perfume.

"Sam told me the kidnapper has been in constant contact," Seth prompted.

"Kind of," Callie explained. "I got the first letter about three months after Kevin was abducted from the hospital."

"How was he taken?" Sam asked.

"A woman dressed as a hospital volunteer simply walked into the nursery and wheeled him out."

Callie's eyes seemed to glaze over with torment as she recounted the incident.

"The hospital's video cameras followed her to the stairwell, then nothing."

"Could they get a description?" Seth asked.

Callie shrugged. "She had short, dark hair. Medium height, slender. It was hard to tell anything more. The videotape wasn't the best quality."

Silently Sam felt a rush of relief wash over him. Lynn had long, strawberry-blond hair and she was on the tall side.

"How old was he?" Sam asked.

"Twenty-six hours and seventeen minutes." Callie smiled uncomfortably. "Sorry, I guess I have so few details about my son that I've sort of obsessed over what little I do have."

"No witnesses?" Seth asked.

"No one saw anything. At least, no one came forward. Jim York, my P.I., has tracked down almost everyone who was at the hospital that day. Employees, patients, visitors, parking lot attendants. No one remembered seeing a dark-haired woman leaving with a newborn."

"The letters started three months later?" Seth asked, though he was looking directly at Sam when he spoke.

Sam knew what his brother was thinking. Kevin had been three months old when he and Lynn started dating.

"Two and a half," Callie corrected. Standing, she walked over to a wooden crate and reached inside. She produced an expanding file folder and brought it over. "This is what I've gotten. Well, actually, they're copies. The FBI has the originals."

Seth picked up each letter, read it, then passed it to Sam. The notes were brief, but informative. The baby was with a family who loved him. The baby was healthy and happy. The baby was growing. The baby had two teeth.

"This is sick," Sam mumbled as he tossed the fifth letter onto the coffee table. "What kind of person would do this?" Sam felt rage surge through him. The letters, the warning, all of it made him want to punch something.

"It's better than not knowing anything," Callie said softly as she wrapped her arms around herself.

"Is there anything familiar about the pattern of writing?" Seth asked.

She shook her head. "Like I told the FBI, there is nothing in any of the letters that I recognize. You've seen them. They're just short sentences. They could have been typed by anyone with a first-grade education."

Seth carefully placed the letters into the folder. "What about the baby's father?"

Callie's expression went blank. "He isn't involved. The authorities cleared him immediately. He wasn't in Montana when Michael was born and at least a dozen people verified his alibi."

He wondered why it was so easy for her to dismiss the boy's father out of hand. "Maybe he had a female accomplice?" he suggested.

Callie's smile was void of humor. "He had a fiancée," she stated flatly. "He left that fact out when we were together. Believe me, he didn't want Michael *before* he was born. I'm sure his feelings didn't change afterward."

Sam felt a rush of sympathy for her. What little he had observed of Callie made him fairly sure that she wasn't the type to think the worst of someone. She gave total honesty and no doubt expected it in return. The guy who got her pregnant was lying slime. *So what does that make you?*

"Who knew you'd given birth?" Seth asked.

"I called my father," Callie answered, then gave a mirthless laugh. "He hung up on me before I could tell him he had a grandson."

Seth seemed to latch on to that information. "Is there any possibility that he—"

Callie held up her hand. "He made it clear from the instant I told him I was pregnant that he wanted nothing more to do with me or my child."

Seth downed his coffee and stood up. "Sorry for the questions, Miss Walters."

"Callie, please. And don't apologize. It's kind of nice to have someone take an interest in the case."

"I don't know what I can do," Seth warned gently.

Callie gave him a warm smile. "Anything you do would be wonderful."

"You coming, Sam?" Seth asked.

"I'd like to ask you something," Callie said before he could answer.

"You go ahead," Sam told his brother. "And thanks."

"No problem," Seth assured him before he left.

The room seemed small and quiet when he was alone with her again. She seemed tentative, cautious, no, vulnerable. And that inspired all his protective instincts.

"Are you okay?" he asked.

"Not really," she admitted. "I've got a proposal for you."

"A proposal?"

Letting her head fall to one side, she peered up at him with those big aqua eyes. "I'm a little spooked by the message from the kidnapper. Since you want me to paint scenes from your ranch, any chance I could stay there for a few days? I'd cut my fees in half."

Panic welled inside of him, tearing him apart. "I—um."

"Never mind," Callie said quickly. "It was a silly proposition. I'll be fine. Besides, Jim was working on a fresh lead recently. It didn't pan out, but apparently the kidnapper doesn't like the fact that I still haven't given up.''

"Your P.I. was on to something?" *Me, maybe?*

"That was a while ago," Callie told him. "It didn't pan out, and I ran out of cash. It's weird that the kidnapper waited so long to warn me off, though. But then, everything that woman does is weird.''

"You haven't done anything recently that might have brought the woman out of hiding?" Sam asked.

"Michael's photograph was shown on that real-crime program a couple of weeks ago. The producers did a computer enhancement showing what he would look like today.''

"Do you have a copy of it?''

Callie seemed surprised by his question. Or maybe it was the urgency he had stupidly failed to keep in check.

She went back to the crate and pulled out a manila envelope. Carefully she pulled out a single page and handed it to him.

Sam's heart raced as he scanned the drawing. Other than the shape of the face, the sketch looked almost nothing like Kevin. The eyes were too wide and the nose was smaller. The hair was shadowed, making it look dark. Kevin was a towhead.

"He's a good-looking boy," Sam said.

Callie shrugged. "If you believe in the accuracy of computer aging.''

"You don't?''

"The only picture I have of my son was taken on the day he was born. Have you ever seen those horrible first pictures? The babies all look the same. I only saw his eyes opened once. They were blue, but all babies are born with blue eyes. He didn't have any hair.''

Callie's chin quivered slightly, so Sam knew she was battling tears. That knowledge wreaked havoc with his conscience. Was he doing the right thing?

''Look at me,'' Callie admonished, wiping unshed tears from her eyes. ''I promised myself that I wouldn't do this. I didn't even watch the program when it aired. False hope is worse than no hope.''

''Callie, I—''

''Go home, Landry,'' she insisted, taking his arm and leading him to the door. ''Give me a call when you want me to go out and sketch at the ranch.''

''But—'' he turned and looked down at her, his mind blurred and confused ''—I'd be a real heel if I left you alone when you're upset.''

She offered a brilliant smile. ''That's sweet, Landry, but I'm tough, remember. And I'm not your problem.''

''I can at least stay until you fall asleep.''

''That would be a very bad idea.''

''Why?''

She rolled her eyes. ''Because right now I'm needy. If you stay another minute, I'll probably do something really stupid, like seduce you just for a few hours of distraction.''

''I would never take advantage of a woman,'' Sam said. ''I'm not that kind of guy, Callie.''

"I know that, Landry. That's what makes you so appealing."

SAM ARRIVED at the Lucky 7 just before two in the morning. It was a short night. He was awakened at five forty-five by Kevin prying open his eyes.

"Morning, pal."

Kevin straddled Sam's body and placed a loud, sloppy kiss on his cheek. His hair was tousled from sleep but his blue eyes were wide with enthusiasm for the day ahead. Sam tickled his neck as he studied the boy. Kevin did bear a slight resemblance to Callie. They were both fair, they both had rounded faces and small lips. But then again, so did a lot of people. There was still the issue of the contact from the kidnapper. That was a point not in Callie's favor. It helped salve his conscience about not telling her of his suspicions. Sam needed to believe he was saving her from the heartache of another false lead.

"Get up!" Kevin demanded, yanking Sam by the hand.

Sam complied. He allowed the small boy to pull him out of the room and down to the kitchen. Shane was already dressed and seated at the table.

"Morning," Sam said as Kevin dropped his hand and went racing to Shane.

"You should have let your dad sleep," Shane told the child. "He had a hot date last night."

"Hot date?" Kevin repeated.

Sam gave his brother a venomous look as he poured himself some coffee, then poured juice into a matching mug for Kevin. "I had a meeting last night."

Shane snorted. "A meeting with a woman that lasts until the wee hours of the morning is a date."

"It wasn't a date."

His brusque insistence earned him a chuckle from his youngest brother. "Why don't you take your juice into the family room, buddy," Shane suggested to the boy. Once he was gone, Shane added, "So was she hot?"

Sam felt his temper rise. "It wasn't a date, you moron."

Shane twisted his shoulder-length hair into a ponytail and secured it with a strap of leather. "What are you getting all testy about?"

"I'm not testy," Sam insisted. "I'm tired and I'm not in the mood to explain myself to you."

"Lighten up, Sam. Okay, so it wasn't a date. But if it was, I'd be happy for you. It's about time."

Sam frowned. "My wife died less than a year ago."

"A wife you didn't love," Shane said pointedly. "If it wasn't for the kid, you'd have divorced that woman a week after the wedding. Which, as I recall, was exactly how long you dated her before you were fool enough to marry her."

"Be quiet! You want Kevin to hear you?"

"The kid can't hear over the blasting television," Shane said. "You've been acting weird for weeks, all tense and secretive. I think you need to get lucky."

"That's because all of your thoughts originate below your belt."

Shane grinned. "Only the good ones."

Sam sighed impatiently. "Don't you have some work to do?"

"In a minute. I'm not trying to make you mad. I'm just pointing out that you've been edgy lately. You devote all your time to Kevin, which is admirable."

"I'm his father."

"Kind of," Shane corrected. "How's the adoption coming?"

Placing his mug on the counter, Sam rubbed his face. He went to the doorway and checked on Kevin. He was seated cross-legged on the floor, hypnotically staring at the television screen. "I've run into a problem."

Shane sat back in his chair and listened as Sam told him about Lynn's deception and his search for the child's biological mother.

"You think this artist is his mother?" Shane asked when he had finished.

Sam shrugged noncommittally. "I'm sending the straw to the lab for testing. I should know in a few days."

"How did you find her?"

"I tracked Lynn from Ohio to Montana. I know she was in Helena for six months. She stayed in a motel until the day Callie's baby was kidnapped."

"Was she pregnant?"

Sam shook his head. "The manager was certain

she wasn't. I didn't find any trace of her for three months, until she showed up here in Jasper with Kevin.''

''Sounds to me like you've got Callie Walters's son.''

''Or Lynn got Kevin from someone else during the three months I can't account for.''

Shane clucked his tongue. ''The kidnapper made contact last night. So maybe Lynn had an accomplice.''

Sam hated to even consider that fact. It put Callie Walters back in the running.

''Maybe, but—'' Sam's comment was interrupted by the telephone. He grabbed the receiver and said, ''Hello?''

''Mr. Sam Landry?'' the voice was low, scratchy and hard to hear.

''Yes.''

''If you don't leave well enough alone, someone will have to die. Maybe the kid.''

Chapter Three

He couldn't get away fast enough, Callie thought the next evening as she pulled her key from her handbag to unlock her front door. Then she saw the shadow of a figure out of the corner of her eye. Half turning in his direction, she felt the first blow. It knocked her to the ground and had her seeing stars. After the second blow, she saw nothing.

SAM HUDDLED with Seth and Shane in the richly paneled office at the Lucky 7. He had managed to get through his day at the office in spite of the ominous morning call. Now he was able to give the problem his full attention.

"You should have hit star-69 instead of calling me," Seth admonished for the third time. "First thing you do now is get caller ID. In the interim, I've been in touch with the Helena PD."

Sam felt a wave of panic. "You didn't tell them about the call, did you?"

Seth let out a breath, clearly exasperated. "No. But I think we should."

"Me, too," Shane opined. "Someone has threatened you, the kid and the Walters woman. You can't keep this under wraps."

Sam frowned and rubbed his hands over his face. "I'm not going to risk telling Callie anything until I have the results of the DNA test. Speaking of which—" he directed his attention to Seth "—I presume you sent the straw to the lab, priority."

Seth nodded. "I'll call in the morning to be sure they expedite the test. But I still vote you should tell her."

"And quick," Shane added.

Sam blew out a breath. "I don't technically have anything to tell." A vision of Callie being crushed by another false lead flashed in his mind. He truly didn't want to be the one to send her over the edge.

His brothers greeted his comment with skepticism.

"I don't!" he insisted. "All I know at this point is that Callie Walters's son is roughly the same age as Kevin."

"C'mon," Shane challenged. "What's the likelihood that the Walters kid was kidnapped a few days before your barren wife showed up in Jasper toting a baby?"

"I can think of at least one other explanation," Sam defended. "Lynn could have adopted Kevin illegally someplace between Ohio and Montana. That would explain the bank withdrawals."

"What withdrawals?" Seth asked.

Sam opened his briefcase and pulled out the neat stack of papers. "I didn't think anything of it, back when she was alive, but Lynn was making regular withdrawals from our checking account the whole time we were married. I dismissed it, thinking she just bought a lot of clothing or something.''

"How much was she spending?" Shane asked.

"A grand. On the fifth of every month.''

Seth whistled. "Lynn was a sharp dresser, but a thousand dollars a month sounds more like blackmail than out-of-control catalogue shopping.''

"I think that nails it," Shane said. "You've got to come clean with the Walters woman.''

Sam gave a firm shake of his head. "Not yet.''

Both brothers began to argue immediately. Sam silenced them by raising his hand. "You didn't spend time with her. If I tell her what I suspect and I'm wrong, I honestly think it would kill her.''

"What will it do to her when she finds out her missing child has been fifty miles away all this time?" Shane asked. "And that you kept him from her even after you suspected the truth?''

Sam closed his eyes tightly and uttered a muffled curse. "I'll deal with that when *and if* I know Kevin is hers.''

"Deal with it how?" Seth asked.

Sam shrugged. "We'll have to work something out.''

Seth scoffed, then gently said, "If she's the kid's mother, you have no rights, Sam.''

"I'm his father.''

"Wrong," Shane said. "Did she tell you who his father was?''

Sam leveled his gaze on his youngest brother. "I don't know that Kevin is her missing son, but no, she didn't mention it."

"What about the birth certificate?" Seth asked. "Isn't that how you found her?"

"Actually, I paid off a clerk in the records office at the hospital where Callie gave birth."

Seth offered a look of censure. "I'll pretend I didn't hear you admit to that felony."

Sam ignored him. Breaching the hospital's privacy was the least of his worries and the most expeditious way to get the information he sought. "Callie left the box for the father's name blank."

"What about the newspaper accounts of the kidnapping?" Seth asked. "Wasn't the father mentioned?"

"No," Sam said. "Which is pretty strange, considering."

"Very strange," Seth agreed. "I'll call the Helena PD and see if there's anything about the father's identity in their reports."

"Thanks," Sam said. "How long will it take for the lab to do the DNA?"

"A week, maybe. More like two to three," Seth explained. "What are you going to do until then?"

"Lay low," Sam answered. "Obviously my making contact with Callie upset someone, though I still don't know how the kidnapper would have known I was taking her to dinner. I'll just have to avoid her until I know one way or the other."

Seth stroked his chin and said, "Could be the kidnapper is close by. Keeps an eye on her comings and goings.''

"Which means it wasn't Lynn," Sam announced.

"Or it means Callie's being watched."

Sam felt a shiver of foreboding dance along his spine. What if his simply making contact with Callie had caused the kidnapper to panic and warn Callie with the news clipping and him by phone? But that didn't mesh unless Kevin was her son. And the only person who could tell him the truth was dead.

Shane was shaking his head, his eyes filled with reproach. Sam was about to defend his position yet again when the phone rang.

"Hello?"

"This is Myrtle, is Sheriff Landry there?"

Sam handed the phone to his brother. Seth's expression stilled and grew serious as he asked questions like "When?" and "Was she hurt?" As soon as he replaced the receiver, he looked at Sam.

"What?"

"It's the Walters woman."

Sam felt his blood freeze in his veins. "What happened?"

"Someone broke into her place."

Sam relaxed a little. "Robbery?"

Seth shook his head. "No one knows yet."

"What does that mean?"

"She was beaten pretty badly. The patrol unit said they found her with her car keys still in her hand. Looks like she was unlocking her door when she was attacked. Still hasn't regained consciousness."

HER EYES FELT as if it would take an act of God to force them open. The immense effort was painful and only partially successful. It took almost a full minute for her vision to clear.

"Welcome back."

"Landry?" she asked, surprised and confused. When she tried to move, her muscles screamed in protest. "Ouch."

"Stay still," he commanded, moving next to her.

Callie looked over at the rails on the bed and then to the IV pole, then finally put the pieces together. "Why am I in the hospital?" *Better still, why are you here?* Her voice sounded weak and scratchy.

Sam's handsome features were a mosaic of concern. Even in the dim light she could see the worried wrinkles at the sides of his eyes and the forced smile on his lips.

"You don't remember?"

Lifting her hundred-pound arm, Callie felt her forehead. Or more accurately, the bandage covering the area where she felt a dull throb. "I remember standing in front of my house getting my keys out. I saw a silhouette, then I saw stars. Then nothing. What happened?"

"Apparently you surprised a robber."

"A robber?" She almost laughed. "Who would try to rob me? I don't have anything of value."

"That might explain why he used you as a punching bag."

Callie drew in a breath and winced. Her chest felt

tight and sore. "Ouch! Please tell me they caught the guy."

"It was a man?" Sam asked.

"I think so. I don't exactly have a clear picture in my head. It's more like an impression." *I have an impression of you, too, and it doesn't include you standing at my bedside offering comfort.*

"Tall, short, fat, thin?"

With great effort Callie pushed herself up into a sitting position. "I don't know. I also don't know why you're here."

"The Helena PD called my brother."

"Which one?"

He gave her a crooked smile. "Seth, the sheriff. He just happened to be out at the ranch when his dispatcher got the call."

"Why did they call Seth?"

"Professional courtesy," Sam answered dismissively. "I guess that since he showed an interest when the threat was tacked to your door, the local cops thought he should be notified when you were found."

"This is too weird," Callie admitted. "I get threatened *and* robbed inside forty-eight hours. If I didn't know better, I'd think you were responsible for this," she said with a smile.

"A definite streak of bad luck," Sam agreed as he averted his eyes. "I've—"

He was cut off by the appearance of a man in a white coat. It took Callie about two seconds to realize

she was about to meet yet another member of his
large clan.

He brushed Sam aside and smiled down at her.
"Chance Landry," he said as he extended his hand.

"The general practitioner from Jasper, right?"

His grin broadened. "Guilty." He lifted a metal
chart from the foot of her bed and began reading.
"Concussion and a laceration that had to be irrigated
and sutured. Multiple contusions to the diaphragm,
negative X-rays."

"In plain English?" Callie pleaded.

"You got whacked in the head. The weapon was
most likely a piece of firewood. The E.R. doc removed several slivers of wood and some dirt. You've
got some bruised ribs, judging from the shape and
location of the bruising, you were kicked repeat-
edly."

Callie felt her stomach churn. "Less *detailed* English, please."

"Wait over there," Chance said to Sam. Once
Sam moved to the far corner of the room, Chance
produced a small penlight and began to check her
pupils.

"How come a general practitioner from Jasper is
examining me in a hospital in Helena?" *Or more
accurately, why is Sam's brother suddenly my at-
tending physician? Did Sam arrange it? If so, why?*
The only explanation was that perhaps Sam wasn't
quite as aloof as he pretended. Except that Sam
hadn't indicated he gave one hoot about her. The

Landry men were confusing under the best of circumstances, which this wasn't.

"We Landrys are like the Musketeers," he joked. "One for all and all for one."

"I barely know Sam," Callie said. "I don't even know why he came to the hospital."

Chance palpated her tender ribs and listened to her lungs and heart. "I'd say you were a very lucky lady."

Nice avoidance move, she noted. Apparently Chance wasn't going to be much assistance in helping her solve the puzzle of his brother. "Forgive me if I don't feel so lucky," Callie said. "What kind of an animal would do this?"

"That's Seth's department," Chance answered, then he called out to Sam. "You're staying here tonight for observation."

Callie groaned. "I don't like hospitals."

"Neither do I," Chance joked. "But you need to have your vital signs checked regularly for twenty-four hours. I'm also going to give you a course of antibiotics just as a precaution."

"Precaution against what?" she asked.

"Your wound was pretty dirty. You don't want to get an infection, it could make the scar much worse."

"Scar?"

Chance smiled as he gently squeezed her wrist. "You've got ten stitches at your hairline. I'll take them out in a week or so."

Callie grimaced. "I can't wait."

"Once you're released, you'll need to take it easy. Is there someone who can look after you?"

"I can ask my neighbor to drop by the house."

Chance and Sam exchanged looks before Sam said, "You can come out to the ranch until you're better."

Callie sensed the invitation was sincere, which was a complete about-face from their previous conversation on this subject. Still, there was something in Sam's voice that didn't gel with his words. She didn't exactly relish the idea of being alone, but she didn't want to impose on this man or his family, either. "That isn't necessary," Callie insisted, forcing lightness to her tone. "I'll be fine at home."

"We can discuss it tomorrow," Sam said.

"You get some sleep," Chance ordered. "I'll be back tomorrow to spring you."

Sam lingered after his brother left. "Do you want me to stay until you fall back to sleep?"

Callie told him no. "You've already done enough. I mean, you've got one brother searching for the robber and another seeing to my medical care." Callie lifted her eyes to his. "Why are you going to so much trouble for a virtual stranger?"

Sam looked away. "It isn't an inconvenience. I'm just glad you weren't hurt more seriously."

"Nice try," she said. "I've been a disaster virtually since we met. A normal man would be avoiding me like the plague." *But you aren't normal,* she mused. Sam was like her own guardian angel, and an attractive angel at that! Her only lingering concern was, Why? Having a gorgeous man seeing to your every need was flattering and pretty close to fairy-tale time. After all that had happened, Callie didn't believe in fairy tales. *Right?* she questioned as she turned and looked at him.

He stood at the window with his back to her. His broad shoulders lifted in gentle rhythm with his breathing. The faint, appealing scent of his cologne countered the sterile smell of the hospital room.

"I'm being practical. You can't paint for me un-less you recover from this. I'm protecting my in-vestment."

"How is this the least bit practical?" Callie chal-lenged. "When you took me to dinner, I droned on about my personal problems. Then I got a nasty note tacked to my door and proceeded to fall apart. Now this. I'd think you'd want to be as far away from me as possible."

"I enjoyed having dinner with you," Sam said after a brief silence.

She let out a frustrated breath. "You scare me, Landry."

He turned and met her gaze. "Why?"

He looked strong, virile and handsome in the soft light. Apparently the thief had failed to bruise her libido. It was annoying to know she found this man attractive when he obviously didn't share her interest. "You aren't normal."

He responded with a sexy half smile he probably didn't even know was sexy. "Why would you say that?"

"You're too...*nice*," she fairly cried. "You barely know me and yet you're here. I'm looking but I can't seem to find your fatal flaw."

"Flaw?"

His eyes darkened for an instant and she was sure she had offended him.

The flash of emotion passed and his smile returned, brighter and more alluring than before. "I have plenty of flaws, Callie."

"Name one," she challenged.

He chuckled softly. "You'll have to trust me on this issue." He retrieved his suitcoat from the back of an orange vinyl chair. "You get some sleep. I'll be back by the time you're released."

Callie spent the remainder of the evening trying to make some sense out of things. Her emotions ran the gamut. She was furious to think someone had attacked her. It didn't make sense, either. Why would someone break into her house when it was obvious that her neighbors were better candidates? The Thompsons next door had a satellite dish that was visible from the street. On the other side, the Grahams' expensive convertible was always parked inside the open garage. What kind of thief would pick her house? Unless he was after something else. But what? Callie didn't have a single thing of value. It wasn't logical.

Neither was the rapt attention she was getting from Sam Landry. Settling against the rather firm mattress, her mind produced a clear, vivid image of the man. Why was such a gorgeous, intelligent, modestly wealthy man acting as her guardian angel? Her platonic guardian angel. He'd walked away after she had all but served herself up on a silver platter. So what was this about? Why was he being so...*perfect?*

Callie alternated between mulling things over and sleeping fitfully until early morning. She was served an inedible breakfast, followed a few hours later by an equally unappetizing-looking lunch just before a cheery nurse came in.

"How are you feeling?" the nurse asked.

"About as good as I look," Callie admitted.

The nurse grinned. "Didn't seem to bother that boyfriend of yours any."

"Boyfriend?"

The nurse planted her hands on her ample hips. "Are you saying that handsome hunk isn't spoken for? Then I'm calling dibs."

Callie smiled. "He's unattached."

The nurse's brow furrowed. "What's wrong with you?" she chided as she strapped on a blood pressure cuff. "A man that fine, well, you don't drag your heels."

"Why did you think he was my boyfriend?" Callie asked as the woman shoved a thermometer into her ear.

"He rushed in here like your life depended on it. Insisted on staying with you until you woke up," she explained. "Had all of us swooning at the nurses' station. Until Dr. Landry showed up."

Sam had rushed to her when she was unconscious? Her heart swelled more than a safe amount. Still, he wasn't acting like a simple doer of good deeds. She only wished she knew why. It did make her smile. "So, what happened when Chance came?" Callie asked.

The nurse melodramatically placed her hand over her heart. "Dr. Chance Landry is a legend in this hospital. He did his residency here."

"Really?"

"Sure. In two years he managed to date every nurse on staff but not one of us could convince him to make a commitment. Heck, I was thrilled when it was my turn to be Mrs. Dr. Landry du jour."

Callie laughed. "I suppose a doctor is still considered a great catch."

"Only if you like living alone," the nurse sighed. "They're married to their jobs first and foremost. Did I hear right? Is yours one of his brothers?"

"He isn't mine," Callie corrected, reminding herself of that fact. No matter how attentive Sam was, she had other things to prioritize, like finding Michael. "But yes, Sam is the oldest brother."

The nurse made a swooning sound. "What I wouldn't give to be lost on an island with the seven Landry men."

"I don't like islands."

The nurse's face flooded with color at the sound of the male voice, then her head whipped around. Chance was standing in the doorway wearing a grin.

"Sorry, Doctor," the nurse muttered before making a hasty exit.

Though there was a definite resemblance,

Chance's style was nothing like Sam's. He wore faded jeans, a denim shirt and a loosely knotted tie. Except for the smile. The smile was apparently a Landry patent.

"How are you doing?" he asked as he grabbed up her chart.

"I have a killer headache, and it hurts when I breathe deeply."

"Then, as your doctor, it is my duty to tell you not to take deep breaths," Chance teased. "Your vitals are stable, but the nurses tell me you didn't get much rest."

"From what I hear the nurses are more interested in you than me."

Chance took her ribbing in stride. "There's quite a nice selection of nurses here."

She laughed. "Doctors, too, I'll bet. So how come you're my treating physician?"

"Sam asked me."

"Why?"

Chance's head came up then, his expression puzzled. "Because I'm a doctor?"

"A doctor from Jasper," Callie pointed out. "I'm trying to figure out why your brother has taken such an...interest in me."

Chance cocked his head to one side. "Now that you mention it, you aren't Sam's type."

She knew she shouldn't ask, but she couldn't help herself. "Really? What is his type?"

"Nonexistent," Chance answered. "Sam lost his wife almost a year ago."

"I know."

Chance wrote a note, then flipped the chart closed and replaced it at the foot of the bed. "I asked one of the nurses to find you some scrubs."

"Why?"

"I thought you'd prefer leaving the hospital wearing something that covered more than that hospital gown."

Callie adjusted the flimsy thing. "Thanks. I guess my clothes were destroyed?"

"Cut off by the E.R. folks. The cops took your sweater for forensics. I can see about anything else."

She waved her hand. "Don't bother. Thanks for thinking ahead."

"That's why I get the big bucks," he quipped. "I'll call the pharmacy and have them send the antibiotics out to the ranch. Are you allergic to penicillin?"

"No. But—"

"Pregnant?"

"No. But please don't have them sent to the ranch. I'm going home." *I'm not sure I can be alone with Sam. Not until I find his flaw. Until then, he's just too damned tempting!*

Chance's expression grew stern. "I don't think it's a good idea for you to be alone. At least not for a few days."

"I wouldn't be comfortable at your place," Callie said. "Besides, I'd probably drown in all the testosterone, with six men under one roof."

"That isn't a problem. Only Shane, Sam and

Kevin live at the ranch.'' Chance's beeper chirped to life. He read the display and said, "A nurse will bring you clothes, and an orderly will take you downstairs as soon as Sam gets here. Call me if your pain gets worse or if you feel nauseous or confused.''

"I am confused,'' she grumbled when he left. "Who is Kevin? Doesn't matter. I'm not going to the ranch.'' She thought about Sam's bedroom eyes and muscular, perfect body. "Head injury or not, apparently I can't be trusted alone with the man.''

Chapter Four

"I found your flaw," Callie grumbled as she got into the car."

"Really?" Sam asked, not sounding the least bit concerned.

"You're bossy," she scoffed. Can't we at least go by my place so I can get some toiletries? There are things from my house that I *need*," Callie pleaded for the third time.

Sam shook his head and continued to drive the smoothly paved highway that connected Jasper to the more metropolitan Helena. "I sent Mrs. Lange to the store to buy whatever she thought you might need immediately."

"Mrs. Lange?"

Sam briefly glanced over at Callie. In spite of the black eyes, the bruised cheek and the bandaged forehead, she was still fabulously attractive. Acknowledging that didn't exactly make things easier.

"Mrs. Lange?" she prompted again.

"She's our housekeeper. She's been at the Lucky

7 since the day my parents moved in. You'll like her. She's blunt like you.''

He heard her expel a breath. From the corner of one eye, he noted that the surgical scrubs were a bit tight. He no longer had to guess about her shape. Every perfect, womanly curve was visible beneath the blue outfit.

Silently he reminded himself that Callie was off-limits. He was taking a big enough risk without complicating matters by allowing his hormones to get the better of him.

"Why are *you* scowling?" she asked. "I'm the one you're dictating to. You didn't ask me to dinner, you told me we were having dinner. You didn't ask me if I wanted to recuperate at your place—you announced it. And you run hot and cold. One minute you're the most kind, attentive person on earth, and the next thing I know you're being bossy. You really are a pain, Landry, anyone ever tell you that?"

"I was not scowling, I was thinking," Sam hedged. "You said your father lived near Helena. Did you call him?"

"No," she said with finality.

"Why?"

"He wouldn't be interested."

Sam felt a surge of anger. "What do you mean? You were attacked for God's sake. A father should care when his child is injured regardless of some long-standing feud. I—"

"Drop it, Landry."

Sam considered the fervor in her proclamation and

then had a thought that sickened him. What if Callie had been abused? What if her father had been the one who impregnated her? That would explain the hostility and the complete lack of contact.

"I'll drop it," he answered solemnly. "Isn't there anyone you're close to?"

She nodded her head. "Of course I have friends, Landry. But why bother them with old news? It's over and done with. I did call Jim York to bring him up to speed. I thought he should know what's been happening, and I wanted to get him back to work."

"You know they haven't caught your attacker," Sam reminded her. When they did, he would love a few minutes alone with the guy. It would give Sam great pleasure doing unto him as he had done unto Callie.

Callie rubbed her arms. His jacket seemed to swallow her.

"I don't think it was a thief."

Sam gripped the wheel a little tighter. "Why not?"

"You saw my street, Landry. I have the only unrenovated building. A *real* thief would have gone someplace else. Someplace that at least looked like it would have a big-screen TV or a stereo worth stealing."

"You think the guy was there to beat you?" He saw her shiver and wished he'd put that a tad more delicately. "I meant, is there someone you think wants to harm you?"

"No. Unless it was the same person who put the

newspaper clipping on my door. Not that I have the first clue what that was supposed to mean. 'Leave it alone' is pretty generic.''

''Have you done anything out of the ordinary recently?''

''Not really. I did call Jim York after I first met you.''

''He's the investigator?''

She nodded. ''I told him I was going to earn a commission and I asked him if he had passed your car on his way out yesterday. He said yes, he'd seen your fancy Jag. Then I had dinner with you, which is very out of the ordinary for me, but I hardly think that would make the kidnapper mad. Other than that, I haven't met anyone new or done anything differently.''

''You didn't speak to anyone else? Think!''

''Not me, but I'm sure Jim probably called Mary. And by the way, please stop giving me orders, I don't like it.''

Sam turned into the driveway in front of the sprawling ranch house his grandfather had built in the shadows of the snow-capped mountains. Ignoring her request, he pressed on, ''Mary?''

''My stepmother,'' she answered. ''This is impressive, Landry. Only three of you live here?''

''It used to be just the two of us, but since Shane came back, he's been living here.''

''Chance mentioned someone named Kevin.''

As if on cue, his son came barreling out of the house and raced down the stairs. Sam was out of the car in time to catch him when he flew into his arms, squealing.

"You're late," Kevin admonished.

Sam glanced over and saw the positively stricken look on Callie's face. His heart stopped. It was over. She recognized him. Forget high-tech DNA, he'd been a fool to think a mother wouldn't know her own child—if Kevin was hers.

"A monster!" Kevin screamed, then buried his face in the crook of Sam's neck.

Wide-eyed, Callie rose slowly and leaned against the car. She looked frail and shaken and her eyes never left Kevin.

"I can explain," Sam began.

She shook her head. "No need." Her eyes fixed on Kevin.

After what felt like an eternity, Sam fairly screamed, "What?"

She forced a small smile. "He's right. I probably do look like a monster."

Relief rushed through him. She didn't stake claim to the child. "Listen, pal," Sam began as he gently pried the boy's face out of hiding. "This is a friend of mine. She isn't a monster. She got hurt."

"She's a monster and I don't like her," Kevin whined.

"Kevin Landry," Sam said his name sternly. "First you will apologize, then you'll remember your manners."

"No!"

Sam experienced that moment of parental horror

when your own child makes you want to disappear into the nearest hole. "Excuse me?" he said more forcefully.

"No, sir!" Kevin countered. He slipped down and raced back to the house, making an exaggerated arc to keep as far away from Callie as possible.

Sam looked over to see her fighting a smile. She shrugged, winced and said, "At least he got the 'sir' part in there."

Sam walked around to the passenger side of the Jag and placed his hand at Callie's elbow. She felt delicate and small in his grasp. How could any man have attacked her? His blood pressure rose yet again.

"Careful on the steps," he cautioned. "Take them one at a time."

"I have a concussion, Landry. Not paralysis. I promise not to take a header on your front porch, okay?"

"I was just trying to help."

"Why don't you try telling me why you kept your son a secret? That would be helpful."

Sam swallowed, preparing yet again for an accusation. "I—um—"

"I've already figured it out," Callie announced when they entered the foyer.

Sam went still, and Callie turned and peered up at him. He expected to see raw hatred. Instead he saw admiration. "You thought if you told me you had a son I'd freak out, right?"

"N-not freak out, exactly."

"I'm okay with it," she assured him. "I'm not

going to throw myself in the dirt and fall to pieces. In fact, I think he's precious.''

A flash of parental pride swelled inside of Sam. ''He's usually a very nice, polite little boy. I don't know what got into him outside.''

Callie scoffed. ''He's what? Two or three?''

''Three.''

''And he sees me with my blood-matted hair, bruised face and black eyes. It's perfectly normal that he would be afraid. Heck, I'll probably scare myself until I've had a chance to clean up. Speaking of which, please point me in the direction of the closest shower.''

''Chance said you couldn't get the sutures wet.''

''Chance doesn't have blood in his hair,'' Callie retorted with determination. ''I'll be careful.''

''I know you will,'' Sam agreed as he led her up to the second floor. He would see to it personally.

THE HOUSE WAS OBVIOUSLY built sometime in the last century, but years of loving care made sure every inch of carved wood was polished to a brilliant shine. The scent of lemon oil permeated the long hallway, which was lined with a half dozen small tables. Each held a period lamp that seemed to bathe the area in a subtle yellowish glow. The house had the kind of warmth her family home had never seen. All along the walls were framed photograph collections. Some were very old, and some were practically brand new. Several were of Sam and his son, but she didn't see any pictures of his late wife. Was that good or bad? She couldn't decide.

Sam gently moved her toward one of the doors. "I'm washing your hair."

"Wrong."

"I'm washing your hair, and I won't hear any more about it."

She stopped. "Excuse me?"

"What part don't you understand?" Sam retorted. He gave her a gentle tug. "You'll do as I say. My motives are pure."

Mine aren't, she thought as she looped her hand through his arm. Knowing that her humor seemed to throw him off balance and to keep from thinking about the horrible attack, she decided to have some fun at Landry's expense. He deserved it. "Will you scrub my back and everything?"

"I see right through you, Callie."

"What does that mean?"

"You say outrageous things to me because you think I won't take you up on them."

"Will you if I beg?" she fairly purred as they stepped into a masculine-looking bedroom with an adjoining bath. She couldn't help but wonder if this was *his* room.

Sam led her into the bathroom and stood behind her. Their eyes met in the reflection of the mirror. Purposefully he slipped his arms around her waist, careful not to apply any pressure. Dipping his head, he positioned his mouth next to her ear. He felt her tense, saw the pulse at her throat quicken.

His eyes were locked on her face. His tongue flicked out and tasted her earlobe. Her lips parted slightly as she sucked in an audible breath. He did it again, watching the effect in her reflection.

"Callie?" He said her name in a whisper.

"Yes?" She hadn't moved an inch.

"Just because I *haven't* doesn't mean I don't want to. I suggest you don't taunt me. I am only human."

"What if I don't want to stop?" she asked boldly, tired of being ordered around.

"Then remember that I do."

Pain replaced her teasing mood. "You started it," Callie said stiffly. "You don't want me, fine. Then keep your tongue to yourself in the future."

"Let's get your hair washed," Sam agreed, stepping backward. "How do you want to do this?"

Callie hid her anger behind a mischievous grin. "Usually I like to be naked when I wash my hair, but since you're here, we'll have to improvise."

"Callie," he warned through gritted teeth.

"Fine." She went to the side of the tub and folded a towel on the floor. Next she sat and gingerly bent backward so that her head and neck were over the edge. "Wash away."

Sam joined her in the small space. In her present position, she knew he could easily make out every inch of her body. Her breasts strained against thin blue fabric. In order to wash her hair, he would have to straddle her body.

Normally Callie enjoyed having her hair washed and fussed over. But there wasn't anything at all normal about the current situation. As Sam lathered a botanical shampoo in her hair, she forgot everything but the feel of his fingers gently massaging her scalp. Somehow the man had managed to turn the harmless act of washing her hair into the most erotic experience of her life.

By the time Sam rinsed away the lather, Callie was breathing heavily. She didn't understand why she was feeling a longing she hadn't felt in years. She had to keep focused on Michael, and Landry was grieving for his dead wife. She didn't want to compete with either of their ghosts.

SAM LEFT HER IN THE bathroom to soak in the tub. Callie was horrified later when she got her first look at the big purple bruises on her side. "No wonder it hurts when I breathe," she whispered. The anger returned. She spent nearly three-quarters of an hour in the warm water. It had a calming and relaxing effect. There was also the added bonus of being clean.

Stepping from the tub, she carefully secured her hair in a towel, then wrapped her body in another one. Wiping the steam from the mirror, she felt a little thrill when she remembered watching as Sam had tickled her earlobe with his tongue. The man exuded sexy.

"And you exude victim," she told her reflection. It would take a gallon of concealer to cover the dark-purple half circles beneath her eyes. Then there was the slightly swollen reddish place on her cheek. She definitely had that wounded raccoon look going on.

She also had no clothes. Callie grabbed up the surgical scrubs and dressed in them again. It took something away from her relaxing soak. She emerged from the bathroom and immediately spotted a tiny face partially visible in the crack of one of the bedroom doors.

Crouching down, she said, "I don't bite."

Her effort was rewarded by the child letting loose with a bloodcurdling scream. He dashed down the stairs yelling, "It's after me! We have to kill it!"

"Yep, he's warming up to me," Callie muttered as she slowly got to her feet.

Chapter Five

Callie watched from the second-floor window as Shane got into a pickup truck and drove off. A few minutes later the housekeeper led Kevin to a sedan and strapped him in a car seat. Sam's Jag was still parked in the drive.

What she wouldn't have given for a sketchpad at that instant. The ranch was situated just at the base of the mountains. The sky was a beautiful shade of blue. Occasionally a wispy white cloud would make its way across the mountain, providing a misty blanket for acres upon acres of evergreens. The Lucky 7 was beautiful. Even the outbuildings to the far left were perfectly maintained. The sun glinted off the glass windows, spraying golden rays into the adjacent field where four horses lazily grazed on the last remnants of late-fall grass. Fencing provided the perfect outline for the serene setting. It reminded her why she would never leave Montana. Clean air and unspoiled beauty appealed to her artist's eye.

Moving to the mirror, Callie fluffed her hair,

frowning at the bandage her bangs could not disguise. Her bruises disgusted her artist's eye.

She made the pencil-post bed, even fluffed the shams before replacing them at the head of the bed. Since Sam hadn't joined her, she deduced this wasn't his room. Shadows on the walls indicated that pictures or posters had once been hung in the room. Now, however, it was without decoration. Just simple wooden furniture, a chair, a dresser and washstand. It must have belonged to one of the now absent brothers.

A little while later she walked into the kitchen and was greeted by Sam and a bottle of gigantic pills. She got some coffee, then joined him at the table. He smelled of soap and subtle cologne. His sleek, black hair was still slightly damp, making it appear even darker. It was hard to believe that towheaded Kevin was going to evolve into an ebony-haired heartbreaker.

Sam passed a prescription bottle to her. "Chance had these sent over. You are to take them three times a day for two weeks."

"Good morning to you, too, and by the way, I can read." Callie glared at Sam, then at the pills, and then she struggled with the childproof cap. Sam reached out to take the bottle from her. His knuckles brushed hers, sending a little jolt through her system.

"There," he said after successfully battling the cap.

"These are as big as my pinkie!" she exclaimed when she saw the size of the pills.

"They aren't an option," Sam told her with fatherly sternness.

"Oh, joy," she grumbled as she fished one out of the bottle.

"Don't act like a baby," Sam warned.

She gave him a pointed stare. "You aren't the one who has to swallow a pill the size of framing lumber."

"The tetracycline will prevent any infection."

"I know," she said as she put the thing in her mouth and then swallowed a large amount of coffee. She shivered as she felt the pill slide down her throat. "*That* was nasty. Speaking of nasty pills, I have a prescription at home I simply have to have." She watched Sam frown, then added, "What did I do wrong now, your surliness?"

"The instructions say you're to take that pill with water. I thought you said you could read."

She gave him a smug smile. "Water is the main ingredient in coffee," she responded sweetly. "How come you aren't at work?"

He shrugged. The action caused his soft cotton shirt to pull taut against the impressive expanse of his chest. The man definitely had a body! Too bad he had an attitude to go with it.

"I'm taking a few days off."

"For me?"

He sat straighter. "You aren't supposed to be alone, remember?" Sam cocked his head to one side and regarded her with conviction in his dark gaze. "I'd like to be your…friend."

"Is that the first time you've ever said that?" she asked. "You nearly choked getting the word out."

A thin line of perspiration formed above his mouth. He blew out a breath. "Don't make this more difficult."

Callie sighed, then wrapped her hands around her mug. "I'll try to behave, but that's going to be difficult since our styles seem to be at cross purposes. I have to find the humor in things or I'd spend every day in tears. You have this tendency toward bossiness, so at times I feel as if I'm in some sort of boot camp. I'm amazed Kevin didn't salute me on command." She paused. "On the other hand, you can be charming and kind and…perfect. You scare me, Landry."

Apparently this wasn't an issue Sam cared to discuss. "Give me a list of what you need from your place."

"You're all work and no play," Callie chided.

His Adam's apple bobbed as he swallowed audibly. "Please try to be serious for a moment so that we can make an appropriate list," he said with sobering sincerity.

Callie reached over and buttoned the top button of his shirt because of his tone. His mixed signals were frustrating. She sensed that he was attracted to her, but obviously that didn't please him. She guessed the ghost of his wife was the problem. And she had no clue how to compete with a ghost. "I'm going with you," she said.

"No way. Chance said you should take it easy for a few days. You will stay here."

"I will not stay here," she retorted, imitating his tone and cadence. "Sitting in your car isn't exactly what I would call taxing," she countered. "Speaking of which, did you have your housekeeper take your son out this morning because of me? You don't need to do that, Landry. I don't freak out around children."

He lowered his gaze. "She was taking Kevin to day care."

"You have a housekeeper and you've taken time off from work and you *still* send the kid to a sitter?"

When his head whipped up, he had a slightly ferocious look in his eyes. Apparently he didn't like to be questioned on his parenting style.

"In case you haven't noticed, this ranch is miles from the closest neighbor. Not that it's your business, but I send Kevin to day care so he can play with children his own age."

Callie raised her hands in mock surrender. "Okay. Sorry, I didn't understand. I think it's great that you're exposing him to other children. More parents should be so astute about their kids' needs."

Sam's expression grew serious. "I'd like to ask you something."

"Sure." She took a sip of strong coffee.

"What's the problem with you and your father?"

Callie almost choked on her coffee. "My father? Why are you asking about my father?"

His dark eyes held hers. "You didn't want to call

him from the hospital, and you refused to list him as next of kin.''

"Because he doesn't consider us kin," Callie said, feeling the pang of sorrow in her stomach. "You may have this big, close *Brady Bunch* family, Landry, but not all of us do.''

"Did he hurt you?''

"Hurt me?''

Sam ran his square fingertip around the rim of his cup. "Did he abuse you?''

Callie laughed with astonishment. "Are you trying to ask me if my father beat me?''

"Actually, I was wondering if your father did something worse than that.''

Callie blinked. "Sex? Are you asking me if my father is some sort of pervert?''

Sam nodded. "You said the two of you had a falling-out when your son was born and I—''

"Have seen too many daytime talk shows," Callie assured him. "My father disowned me when I shamed him by getting pregnant outside of marriage. To make matters worse, I refused to place the baby up for adoption.''

Sam was staring at her. "He didn't want to know his own grandchild?''

Callie shook her head. "He wasn't interested. He was more worried about his reputation in the community.''

"What about when the baby was kidnapped?''

Callie's expression hardened. "He actually suggested that it was for the best. Now do you understand why I don't communicate with my father?"

"I suppose," Sam muttered under his breath. "I didn't mean to upset you." He reached out and touched her hand.

Callie offered a weak smile. "You didn't upset me."

"Are you sure?"

She nodded.

"Good. Mary called here early this morning."

"My stepmother?" Callie asked, surprised. "How did she know I was here?"

"Apparently she heard about the attack, called Seth and Seth told her you were here."

"Mary is very sweet."

"How does she handle the feud between you and your father?"

"Diplomatically," Callie answered. "After the baby was born, Mary helped me. She was as devastated as I was."

"Really?" Sam asked.

It was Callie's turn to lower her eyes. "Unlike my father, Mary acknowledged her grandchild. She loaned me the money to put the down payment on the firehouse and she found Jim York for me."

"Did she give you money every month?"

Callie lifted her eyes to his handsome face. "Like an allowance? Of course not. Mary got the money for the loan by selling off some stock her first husband had left her. There's no way that my father would permit her to use his money to help me on a monthly basis. I'm no Landry, but I do earn a living.''

"I had to ask," Sam said. "Now let's make that list."

"I'm going with you."

"You're staying," he insisted.

"I am going," she announced, matching his stern tone.

They glared at each other for a full minute before Sam relented and said, "Get dressed and we'll go to your place."

SAM WAS DISTRACTED during the drive to Callie's place. There were some major loose ends that weren't coming together. If Kevin was Callie's son, who was Lynn paying the thousand dollars a month to? He'd like to meet the stepmother, Mary, just to get a feel for her. But it didn't make sense for Mary to be involved in the kidnapping. Not if she had supported Callie. Callie's father was a possibility, but why would the man arrange a kidnapping of his own grandchild, then not reconcile with his daughter? Sam needed to know who the child's biological father was. That would mean gaining Callie's confidence. That would mean spending more time with her.

That concept scared Sam. For all his bravado, he was incredibly attracted to Callie. She was warm, funny, honest and stunningly beautiful. Keeping her at arm's length would be difficult. *What am I doing? What if she spends more time around Kevin and sees or hears something familiar? What if I'm the one responsible for her beating? What if I've put everyone, including Kevin, in danger? I'll have to find a way to protect them both.*

"What are you doing?" Callie asked.

"Huh?"

She pointed out the window. "You just passed my house."

Sam silently chided himself as he made a U-turn. "I guess I was daydreaming."

"Do you do that often while you're driving? If so, I'll be taking my own car from now on."

"I'll have you know I'm a very competent driver."

"Bully for you," Callie teased.

Sam parked, then watched her expression stiffen as she took in the crime-scene tape and the blood spatters visible even from where he parked.

"I'm glad I don't remember much of what happened," she whispered as she unlocked the door.

He watched her eyes fill, then silent tears spill down her cheeks as she took in what was before them. He didn't know exactly what to do. He ended up placing one arm around her and pulling her gently against his side so that she could cry it out. She did so in silence, then stepped out of his embrace to go inside.

The room was in shambles. Her paintings were strewn all over the place, as were her art supplies. "Whoever did this was looking for something," he remarked.

Callie glanced up at him. He saw remnants of fear and pain melded in her green-blue eyes, and it took all his willpower not to pull her back into the comfort of his arms.

"I don't know what," she said as she righted a chair. "It isn't as if I have anything of value."

"No jewelry? No bonds?"

She cast him a sidelong look. "I keep my diamonds under the mattress and my vast stock portfolio in the freezer. Or is it the other way around?"

"I suggest you take this seriously."

Callie glared at him. "I took it seriously when the chief of staff came in and told me my son had been kidnapped. I took it seriously when the FBI suggested I move on with my life. I even took it seriously when the cops suggested I join a support group for parents of murdered children. So don't lecture me on taking things seriously, Landry." Her head dipped for a moment, then her shoulders straightened and she said, "The closest thing I have to a valuable is my mother's wedding ring."

He followed Callie to the loft on the second floor. It, too, was ransacked. He helped her push the mattress back onto the pedestal. Stepping over a broken lamp, Callie reached beneath a slashed quilt for a simple wooden box. "Right here," she said as she produced a plain gold band. "What kind of thief cuts up a quilt but leaves this?"

"A stupid one?" Sam suggested.

Callie's brows drew together. "Does this make sense to you? I mean, whoever did this couldn't have been after valuables. I don't have a microwave or a VCR. So why go to this much trouble?''

"Maybe he was mad because you didn't have anything worth stealing,'' Sam offered.

"Did you see the bloody footprint in the studio?''

Sam nodded.

"He tracked my blood inside, which means he hit me before he came in.''

"You think he wanted to hurt you?''

He watched her shiver and hug her arms around her small frame before she gave a tiny nod. "That's the only scenario that makes sense. But someone whacking me with a hunk of firewood is absurd. I don't have enemies.''

"What about the kidnapper?'' Sam said.

She looked up at him with eyes that were an open wound. "Why would the person who took my son want to hurt me after all this time?''

"Didn't you tell me that your private investigator had a possible lead?''

Callie nodded. "But it didn't pan out. Come downstairs with me. I'll show you Jim's last letter.''

He followed her back to the first floor and helped her create a path through the piles of canvases and broken furniture.

"This is too weird,'' Callie said.

"What?''

"It's gone. Everything is gone.''

He came up behind her and glanced over her shoulder. She was holding an empty file folder. "*What*, specifically, is gone?''

She ran her fingers over the empty file in a haunted caress. "Everything. My son's birth certificate. The photograph that was taken in the hospital. Copies of the police reports and every lead Jim has worked on."

Hearing the catch in her voice, Sam wrapped his arms around her. He felt the silent sobs racking her body. More than that, he felt incredible anger. Who was tormenting this woman? And why? Most of all, was it his fault? Silently he vowed to do anything in his power to keep her from being hurt again.

Anything but give up Kevin.

Chapter Six

Following Callie's instructions, Sam drove to a trailer park just north of Helena. Given the rather run-down appearance of the trailers, he understood why York needed to work upon payment in advance.

He parked in front of a unit that was rusting at the roofline. A dog of indeterminate origin began to bark excitedly as he strained against the frayed rope tied to a precarious railing at the front of the trailer.

Maybe Sam had seen too many TV detectives, but the man who emerged to greet them didn't exactly fit his picture of a private investigator. This guy was small, almost frail looking. Obviously he refused to acknowledge his progressing baldness because he had a rather thin comb-over covering his scalp.

Sam and Callie got out of the car and Callie greeted the man with a warm—if weary—smile.

He scratched the front of his T-shirt, which was stained with some flesh-colored substance, then he gave Callie a hug. His faded green eyes were locked on Sam. "I hear you've had a rough few days," York commented.

Callie touched the freshly applied bandage on her forehead. "It hasn't been my best week."

"Who's your friend?" York asked, cautiously.

Sam extended his hand and said, "Sam Landry."

York's eyes seemed to flash with some sort of recognition, but he stood firm on the steps. "What can I do for you?" he asked. "You want me back on the payroll?"

"Soon," Callie promised, then she explained that she needed copies of all his reports and letters.

"I'll have to mail them to you," York said, still standing his ground.

Sam thought it was odd that the man didn't have the manners to invite his client inside. Then, after taking a closer look at the trash strewn around the yard, he figured York probably wasn't the best of housekeepers.

Callie was frowning.

"I can make the copies at my office," Sam offered. "I'll send the originals back to you by courier. They will only be out of your possession for a few hours."

York stroked his chin with one small hand. Sam would have loved to ask how such an unmanly man had chosen his particular profession. When York hesitated, Sam moved closer to use his height to intimidate York. It must have worked, since York told them to stay put, then disappeared back into the trailer.

"Where did you find this guy?" Sam asked in a whisper. Not that he had to whisper. With York gone, the dog had returned to barking loudly.

"My stepmother," Callie answered softly. "I know he doesn't make a great first impression," she admitted. "But he was willing to work cheap, and he's the best I could afford."

"Maybe he's cheap for a good reason," Sam muttered just as York returned carrying a messy stack of papers and envelopes.

"You'll have this back to me, right?" York asked as he craned his neck to meet Sam's gaze. "I don't make a habit of loaning out my files." He turned his attention to Callie and his expression softened a little. "But for you, missy, I'll make an exception."

"Thanks," Callie fairly gushed as she accepted the papers, which Sam immediately relieved her of.

"My courier will be here before dark," Sam announced, and turned back toward the car.

Callie lingered just a minute before joining him in the vehicle. She reclaimed the stack and began looking through it.

"Is everything there?"

She gave him a questioning look. "Of course. Why wouldn't it be?"

"I think your investigator is an incompetent slob."

Her eyes widened. "Do say what you think," she scoffed. "You are completely off base, Sam."

He stopped in mid-Y-turn and met her gaze. "That's the first time you've done that."

"Done what?" she asked.

"Used my name."

She appeared flustered and instantly averted her eyes. "I'm sorry. I seem to have forgotten that in essence I'm your employee, and I didn't mean to overstep—"

"I don't recall complaining," Sam said. Smiling, he drove out of the trailer park, wondering why hearing his name on her lips was so pleasant.

THE OFFICES OF SILLS, Cartwright and Hingle in Jasper were impressive. Callie marveled at the modern construction, the incredible use of light and floating staircases. She also noted that the receptionist greeted Sam with great deference and a touch of confusion.

"What did you do to her?" Callie asked as he steered her inside an office bearing his name.

"Who?"

"The receptionist. I thought she was going to genuflect when we walked in."

Sam shrugged. "I never noticed."

"Maybe you should start," Callie muttered, looking around. "You do need artwork. This is a beautiful office, but it's a little on the sterile side."

Sam sat in a large leather chair behind an impressive mahogany desk. It didn't surprise Callie that his desk was neat as a pin. He probably left standing orders to have it dusted hourly. The only thing of a personal nature she saw was a framed photo of Sam and his son on the credenza to the right of his desk. While he was on the phone ordering some poor soul to make copies for him, she went to the picture and picked it up.

Kevin was a handsome little boy. His hair was almost white, his eyes an interesting shade of blue. She felt her chest tighten as she ran a fingertip across the image.

"What are you doing?"

Sam's thundering tone almost made her drop the photograph. "Geez, Landry. You nearly gave me heart failure. You don't have to yell, I'll wipe off the fingerprints."

Callie used the hem of her sweater to polish the glass, then set the picture in precisely the same place.

"I didn't mean to startle you," he said in a more reasonable tone.

"Yeah, right," Callie breathed as she primly sat in one of the chairs opposite the desk. Some frantic woman Callie guessed was his secretary came hustling in.

"Good afternoon," she said to Callie as she hurried out with Jim York's reports under her arm.

"Haven't you ever heard of introductions?" Callie asked.

Sam blinked. "Who? Elizabeth?"

"You could have at least given her two seconds for me to say hello and thank her."

"For what?"

Callie glared at him. "For a smart man, you can be so clueless. I'm sure it isn't in her job description to make copies for me."

"Her job description is whatever I make it," Sam countered. "I need to return a few of these calls."

While he was on the phone, Callie examined the bare walls and made a mental note that they were painted a dull gray. She rubbed her sore ribs as she walked around the room, getting a general feel for the place. It was obvious that the room needed paintings of varied dimension. One wall was nothing but floor-to-ceiling window, so it couldn't handle a painting. The area on the credenza wall was at least 20 feet. A single painting would disappear in such a large space. The third wall had another consideration. Low mahogany file cabinets went part of the way up the wall.

She wasn't aware Sam had gotten off the phone until she heard a gentle knock on the door, followed by Sam brusquely saying, "Come in."

Elizabeth was struggling to carry the heavy load of the originals and the copies. When Callie went to her aid, Sam stepped forward and took them. Callie smiled, feeling silently proud of her small victory. Maybe she should tell Elizabeth how Sam acted with his son. Apparently, no one in the office knew how loving and kind he could be. She wondered if they would see him as she did.

Elizabeth's face showed total shock.

"Her ribs hurt," Sam dismissed, then he turned to put the stuff on his desk.

"Don't you have something to say?" Callie prompted quickly.

"Like what?"

Callie indicated Elizabeth with a motion of her head.

Sam gave Callie a withering look, then turned to his secretary and said, "Thank you."

"N-no problem," Elizabeth returned. "I've called the courier service, and they'll be here in less than a half hour to pick up the originals."

"Thanks," Callie said as she took the woman's hand and grasped it for a second.

"Thank *you*," the woman whispered back. "I don't know who you are, but come back soon."

Once Elizabeth left, Callie turned to find Sam scowling at her.

"What?" she asked innocently.

"You've got me thanking my support staff for doing as I tell them. What's next, a four-day work-week?"

Callie gave him an exaggerated look of surprise. "Don't look now, Sam, but you made a joke."

He made a sound very much like a growl before he turned his attention to the files in front of him. "None of this stuff is in order."

"Stop grousing," Callie admonished. She rose, then went around next to him and began sorting through the pages.

Even with two poorly concealed black eyes and a bandage on her forehead, she was beautiful. He hated himself for noticing such a thing. His last foray into jumping into a relationship quickly had left him in a horrible marriage, made tolerable only by Kevin.

Sam pressed his fingers against his temple as she

shifted pages in front of him. He couldn't think of Callie in those terms. If it turned out that she wasn't Kevin's mother, she'd hate him for his pretext. If she was Kevin's mother, she'd hate him, period. No. Callie, as appealing as she was, was definitely off-limits.

"What was that?" Sam asked, just as she slipped one of the documents beneath her sweater.

"Nothing pertinent," Callie insisted.

One look into her eyes and Sam knew she was lying. He held out his hand, palm up. "Let me see it."

"No."

He let out a frustrated breath. "I'm trying to find out who is threatening us. I can't do that without *all* the information."

Her expression stilled. "*Us?* Threatened *us?*"

"You," Sam corrected quickly. "I meant you."

"I think you're fibbing."

"Fibbing? Why would I fib? Besides, stop making this about me. It's about you hiding whatever it was you hid."

Her eyes filled with pain and something else as she slowly pulled the rumpled document from its hiding place. "You have to swear to me that you won't tell a soul about this."

"Callie?" He felt a surge of impatience as he said her name.

"Swear."

"Fine," he breathed. "I swear."

She handed him what turned out to be one page of a report by the Helena PD. It provided full exoneration for a man named David Leary. The name was vagu   miliar, but he couldn't place it. "The baby's father?"

Callie nodded but kept her eyes lowered. "You have to understand that while it does take two to tango, I knew nothing about Brittany Johnson when David and I..." Her voice trailed off.

"Brittany Johnson of Johnson Luxury Automobiles? Of Johnson Auto Mart? Of Johnson everything else?" he asked.

Callie nodded.

"I didn't know he was engaged to marry her."

Sam felt his blood boil. He had known Brittany Johnson for years. She was a spoiled, self-centered beauty queen. He was sure he had met her husband at some charity affair. Had he known David was the man who had gotten Callie pregnant then dumped her, he would have done something other than offer a handshake. "Why are you apologizing?"

She lifted her face to his. "It was wrong. But you need to know that my father was very strict. I spent twelve years in a private Christian school. I was probably the most naive twenty-seven-year-old in the world."

"So that makes you solely responsible for getting pregnant?"

She shook her head. "It's more complicated than that."

"How?"

Callie wrapped her arms around herself and looked

as if she was on the verge of tears. "Can we not talk about this, please?"

Sam wanted to press her, but seeing the pain she was reliving made that impossible. No matter how this ended, she'd be hurt. He didn't want to add to it.

"Okay. Let's take this stuff back to the ranch. I'd like to have dinner with Kevin before he leaves."

"He's leaving?" Callie asked. "Not because of me, I hope. I'm perfectly well enough to go home and—"

"You're staying at the Lucky 7," Sam announced. "I decided to send Kevin to stay with my cousin Cade and his family until we find out who is tormenting you." *Besides, I can't risk you spending too much time with him.*

DINNER WAS an interesting undertaking. Callie had never eaten a meal with a child underneath the table. It was a compromise. The boy would only eat with the monster if he could stay on the floor in his protected place so the monster couldn't kill him.

Sam seemed mortified by his son's behavior. Callie found it funny. Not even the coaxing of his uncle Shane could convince Kevin to come out from the sacred safety of his protected place.

Callie enjoyed Mrs. Lange's meal of stuffed chicken breasts, which was enhanced by Shane's conversation. She found Shane to be much more relaxed than his brother.

"You hurt yourself," she commented to Shane

when he reached for the biscuits and the action revealed a terrible bruise at his wrist.

"He does that on purpose," Sam said. "Always has. When we were little, he would cover himself in bruises, then blame one of us."

"You'd cover me in bruises," Shane corrected.

"We never hit you hard enough to give you bruises. I'm glad to see you're still practicing your favorite childish method of attention-getting behavior. Perhaps you'd be more comfortable on the floor with Kevin," Sam said.

"Yes! Yes! Come down here!" Kevin cried with absolute joy.

"Don't suppose there's room down there for me?" Callie asked.

"You're the monster! I'll melt you and make you die if you come down here!"

"Kevin!" Sam warned between gritted teeth.

Callie raised her hand to silence him, then mouthed the words, *Leave him alone.*

When Callie finished her dinner, she began to clear the table.

"Mrs. Lange can do that," Sam said.

"So can I," she responded sweetly. "And so can you, unless you get some sort of thrill by being served."

Secretly Callie was pleased when Sam wordlessly rose and helped her clear the dishes. When they were finished, he insisted he'd helped only to give Mrs. Lange a chance to pack, since she was going to take

Kevin to Cade and Barbara's, then visit a sister she had near there.

"Are you sure you want to do this?" he asked his housekeeper when she returned to the kitchen carrying a small suitcase and a dinosaur backpack. Callie felt one of those pangs. Was Michael into dinosaurs? Did he have a favorite food or toy?

"I'm sure."

"Is something wrong?" Sam then asked Callie.

Forcing a smile, she shook her head. "Of course not. That was a great meal. I guess I'm just tired." To add realism to her lie, she gently touched her bandage.

Sam's expression grew concerned. "I'm supposed to call Chance if—"

"I'm just tired. I'll take my pills, call it a night." Callie's smile was genuine when she looked at Mrs. Lange. "Thank you very much for your hospitality."

"Come back anytime," she insisted. "Good for all of us to have a woman under roof. Reminds me of the old times." She stopped and reached out for Shane as he entered the kitchen. "Someday they'll be back, right, Shane?"

He shrugged. "Maybe."

"They?" Callie asked.

"It isn't important," Sam said.

"Nothing, really," Shane added.

"They are liars, both of them," Mrs. Lange said as she buttoned her coat. "Miss Pricilla left and Mr. Caleb, the old fool, took off after her. Haven't heard from either of them since."

"Pricilla and...?" Callie asked.

"My parents," Sam said. "I'm going to go say goodbye to my son."

"I've got a mare to check on," Shane announced.

Mrs. Lange was smiling when both men fled. "I can clear a room, now can't I?"

"*Both* parents deserted them?" Callie asked, horrified.

Mrs. Lange shrugged. "Pricilla went off with another man. Caleb got it into his head that he was going to track her down and drag her back if necessary. The old fool probably had a heart attack on some remote mountain pass, and in a hundred years or so they'll find his bones. Least then the boys can put him to rest."

"And the mother?"

"When she announced she was leaving, you coulda dropped me with a feather. I thought they had worked out their problems, but I guess not. An unsigned card shows up here on birthdays and holidays. But apparently the missus doesn't want contact with her boys. Didn't even come back when Clayton got into that trouble. Which—" Mrs. Lange's tone gained conviction "—was completely wrong. We'll get him out of jail soon. He's no killer. I know that boy."

"If you're finished doing the family laundry for the benefit of Miss Walters," Sam grumbled rather harshly as he reentered the room, "Kevin is ready to go."

The housekeeper gave Callie a wink and said,

"Don't let him fool you. He barks but he doesn't bite."

When the Landry family all escorted Kevin to the car, Callie went up and took a soaking bath. The entire day had been an emotional roller-coaster, and she wasn't sure if she had hit bottom or was perched atop the next big hill.

Mrs. Lange had left her horse pill and a large glass of water on the bedside table. Callie took the pill, then went to her purse and retrieved her birth control pills. She took them to keep her skin clear, but she didn't want anyone to see them for fear of giving off the wrong impression.

Callie removed her robe and was almost in bed when she heard the medley of sirens, then saw the parade of emergency vehicles, lights strobing, coming up the drive. She slipped her robe back on and bolted for the front door.

She got there in time to see a paramedic handing Kevin off to Sam. The little boy's eyes were red from crying, but he seemed calmed the moment he was placed in his father's arms.

"What happened?" Callie asked when she joined Shane, Sam and Seth on the steps. She could see unshed tears in Seth's eyes.

"Take him inside," Sam said to Shane as he passed off a now calm Kevin.

"What?" Callie asked more urgently.

Seth's voice cracked with emotion when he said, "Mrs. Lange is dead."

Chapter Seven

Callie made coffee while Seth called the other brothers. Sam and Kevin spent time alone together upstairs. She couldn't believe that she'd been talking to the woman no more than an hour ago, and now Mrs. Lange was dead.

Seth hung up the phone and rubbed his face. "That was hard," he said as he accepted a cup of coffee from her.

Sam came into the room then, looking haunted. "Kevin is asleep," he said. "But I dug out the baby monitor just in case he wakes up in the night. How much did he see?" Sam asked Seth.

"We got lucky there," Seth answered. "There were two photographers nearby in the woods when the shot was fired."

"She was shot?" Callie asked, aghast.

Seth nodded. "A single rifle shot through the windshield."

"God. Kevin," Sam whispered. "I can't believe he witnessed a murder."

"His car seat was in the back, so he didn't see anything," Seth assured him. "The car slowed before going off the road. Kevin doesn't seem to be hurt. One of the shutterbugs got him out of the car on the opposite side while the other tried CPR on Mrs. Lange. I think Kevin was more scared than anything."

"How awful for him," Callie said as she absently placed a hand on Sam's shoulder. "Shouldn't someone be sitting with him?"

"I'll go," Shane offered.

"Thanks," Sam told his brother.

Seth stood and swallowed his coffee in a single gulp. "I've got to get back to the scene."

"Can't someone else take over?" Callie asked, seeing the hurt and reluctance in the man's expression.

Seth shook his head, grabbed his hat and jacket and slowly walked away to do his job.

Sam picked up his mug, took one look at the coffee and placed the mug back on the table. "I need something a little stronger."

He went into the den and poured himself a rather generous bourbon. Over the rim of the glass he saw Callie enter the room. Her expression looked so…concerned. "I don't think I'm in any shape to be great company right now. I should never have let Mrs. Lange take Kevin."

Callie moved, but it was in the wrong direction. She stepped closer, until she was very nearly caught in the vee of his thighs where he leaned against the desk. "When Michael was taken, I felt responsible too. Then I just wanted someone to hold me. I wanted to feel something other than excruciating pain."

Sam swallowed another sip of his bourbon. "Mrs. Lange has been a part of this family since my parents got married. I can't imagine this house without her."

Callie stepped closer. He could hear the gentle rustle of her nightgown, smell the faint floral scent of soap on her skin. She was right. He suddenly had an overpowering urge to hold her. And to be held. That was a very dangerous notion, he reminded himself. He would be a liar if he didn't acknowledge his growing attraction to the woman. But he needed to keep sight of the big picture.

"I think you'd better go," he told Callie.

"Nope," she said softly. "You've been there for me all week. Now it's my turn to return the favor."

His brain was being pulled in completely opposite directions. He had to keep his distance. Even if it meant shoving Callie out of the room, that was what he needed to do. However, the feel of her small body, the sound of her even breathing, everything about her seemed to be overwhelming him. He looked down at her upturned face and saw only her inner beauty. He looked into his own soul and saw only raw need. A very bad combination, but one he couldn't or didn't want to ignore.

Sam slipped his arm around her narrow waist and pulled her to him. Taking one last sip of his drink, he placed it on the table at the instant he felt her palms flatten against his chest. His mind cleared of every thought except her. His good intentions and logic failed him as he watched her lips part slightly. That simple gesture was all it took.

"This isn't a good idea," he whispered against her soft lips.

"Every now and then it's good to do the wrong thing," she whispered back. "Otherwise, we'd all be perfect, and being perfect is no fun."

Sam pulled her closer. "Then, let's get this out of the way, so we can both go back to striving for perfection." Bending at the waist, he leaned forward until his lips barely grazed hers again.

Wide-eyed, Callie experienced the first tentative motions of the kiss through the haze of her desire. As the pressure from his mouth increased, growing slightly more insistent with each passing second, she found herself bombarded with an artillery of conflicting emotions. Her brain struggled to sort out curiosity, desire and just the faintest bit of apprehension.

His hands moved slowly, carefully to her hips. His strong fingers slipped beneath the fabric of her robe and came to rest just beneath the swell of her rib cage.

Her mouth burned where he incited fires with a gentle prodding of his tongue. An involuntary gasp rose in her throat at the heady new sensations pulsing through her system. When he moved closer yet, the feel of his thighs encasing her was almost as intoxicating as the kiss itself. The heat from his mouth washed over her entire body, until every nerve ending tingled with a fierce life of its own.

Fortified by her newly awakened desire, Callie moved her hands across the vast expanse of his chest, around the taut muscles, until she was able to feel the solidness of his back. Arching herself slightly, she held her breath in anticipation of something unknown.

Whatever she'd expected, it wasn't the knocking sound that suddenly reverberated through the house. Sam all but jumped away from her, his breath coming in deep, ragged spurts.

"Um." Shane cleared his throat. "The little guy wants you and I've got to go down to the barn and check on one of the mares' legs."

Without a word, Sam brushed past her. She kept her head down, embarrassed that Shane had caught them in the act.

And what a delicious act it had been, she thought as she made her way back to the kitchen. His kiss had awakened parts of her she thought were long dead. For that brief time, she had felt truly alive. Now, she felt truly perplexed as she went about washing the coffee mugs and setting up the pot for the morning.

Callie brushed her hair out of her eyes and listened to the quietness of the house. She wasn't the least bit tired. Not with her brain moving in so many directions. She felt sorrow for the loss of the housekeeper, even though she hadn't really gotten a chance to know Mrs. Lange well. Horror was the only adjective she could think of, knowing Kevin had witnessed a murder. The poor little boy.

Then she turned her attention to the way it had felt to be in Sam's arms. Though she wasn't fond of his bossiness, she really could find no other faults. She wondered what her life might be like if she had met Sam Landry instead of David Leary.

But that wasn't the way it had worked out, she reminded herself as she climbed the stairs.

On the way back to her room, she peeked into Kevin's. The little boy was sound asleep. Sam gently stroked his tiny hand. Her breath caught in her throat as she soundlessly watched father and son. She hoped Michael had such a loving father figure. She desperately needed to believe that.

Sam turned and caught her gaze. Quietly he slipped off the bed and came toward her. He took her hand, then pulled the door to Kevin's room partially closed.

''Is he okay?'' she asked in a whisper.

Sam nodded. He continued to hold her hand as he led her toward her bedroom.

Callie was thrilled just to have her hand in his. The man had probably had one of the worst days of his life, yet all she could think about was how she had felt when he'd kissed her—as if she was part of the world for the first time since Michael had been taken.

''What's the problem?'' Sam asked when they entered her room. ''You look as though you're about to cry.''

Peering up at him, she said, "I think I am."

"Seth said it was quick," Sam assured her. "I'm holding on to that thought."

Callie reached up and cupped his cheek in her palm. Here he was, trying to comfort her, when he was the one who had suffered the loss. "I feel…strange."

"Why?"

"Your kiss did something to me. It proved to me that I am still alive."

Sam winced. "I was out of line."

Callie took his hand and led him to her bed. "No you weren't." She had lowered her voice to a mere whisper. She felt the edge of the bed at the back of her legs. "When David dumped me for Brittany, I thought I could never feel like this again. I've been too afraid of being hurt again. Your kiss changed that for me. So, would you do it again?"

"Callie?" he breathed.

She saw the conflict in his dark eyes, and it almost quashed her bravado. "We're consenting adults. I like you a lot. All I'm asking for is a kiss. I know you're still grieving for your wife."

Sam seemed to struggle with his conscience for a moment before reaching out and whispering, "I'm not grieving, Callie, but I haven't been with a woman since my wife died. I'm not sure I can stop at just a kiss."

She arched herself against him and said, "I'm not sure I want you to."

Her lashes fluttered against her cheeks as anticipation gripped her.

Sam lifted his head, held his breath and went still. "Callie, you have to be sure. I don't want to hurt you more than you already have been."

"I," she began softly as her small hands moved to his chest, her palms flattening against him, "am *completely* sure."

His body shivered involuntarily at her touch. He was afraid to move, afraid he might somehow break the spell.

"Tell me what you want, Callie."

He saw the raw emotion in her eyes, everything from fear to desire. He prayed desire would win out.

"You," she said on a whisper. "I want you, Sam."

He framed her face in his large, warm hands. He felt her shiver as the tips of his thumbs grazed her lips.

He kissed the corners of her mouth as his hands glided down her spine to her hips. When her arms entwined around his neck, Sam lifted his head and looked into her eyes.

"Are you sure?" he asked.

"Very."

At Callie's word, urgency surged through Sam, setting fire to his blood. Scooping her up in his arms, he lowered her to the bed. He set her down amid the assortment of pillows and settled next to her, arranging her hair to grant him access to the sweet skin of her throat. He kissed, nibbled and tasted. She responded by kneading the muscles at his shoulders and twisting her small body against his. Her actions turned his stomach to liquid and caused an unrelenting ache in his lower body.

Fanning his fingers against her flat stomach, he could feel the effect his kisses were having. His mouth hungrily found hers. She made a small sound against his lips when he moved his hand higher, his knuckles brushing against the underside of her breast. Callie caught his head between her hands; her fingers raked through his hair. He dropped a path of kisses to the hollow of her throat, then explored every inch of her collarbone with his mouth. Catching the lapel of her robe between his teeth, Sam pulled it off her shoulder.

He heard her suck in a breath when his hand moved up to close possessively over a breast. He could feel her taut nipple straining against his palm. He squeezed gently.

Lifting his head, satisfaction spilled through his system when he saw the flush of desire on her cheeks. He captured her lower lip with his mouth, tugging gently as his hand slipped beneath the silky fabric of the gown. Cupping her breast in his hand, he kissed her hard as his thumb teased her nipple. Her response became more urgent as she pressed against him.

Her hands tore at his shirt, pushing the fabric down to trap his arms. Sam lifted away from her long enough to shed the shirt and to look at and admire his prize. Her nightgown had worked its way to her waist, and he caressed her with his eyes. It was a heady experience, looking down at her. Her erratic breathing and desire-glazed aqua eyes were almost enough to send him over the edge.

Caging her with his arms, Sam dipped his head and placed a hard kiss against her open mouth. His tongue teased hers, then moved lower.

She moaned in earnest when his mouth closed over one breast. He kissed the soft valley between her breasts, then alternated his attention between them.

"Sam," she said on a rush of breath. "Sam, please."

He lifted his head, and she arched against him, communicating her need. Her fingers moved through the hair on his chest, until she discovered his nipples. Lifting her head from the pillow, Callie kissed him as he had kissed her. He watched her as her hands eagerly explored the contours of his body. They slipped around him, then moved lower. Callie held his hips firmly against hers. It was his turn to moan.

Catching her chin with his finger, Sam tilted her face toward his and kissed her passionately as he used his knee to spread her legs. He settled against her, feeling smugly male when she reacted to the unmistakable sign of his desire.

He wanted this moment to last forever. He felt her need, and it rivaled his own. Everything else in his life evaporated in a swirl of passion. Her hands molded to his hips, as she matched his rhythm. Slowly, he slid his hands down her side, stopping briefly to explore the soft weight of her breasts.

"Sam," she pleaded against his mouth.

He brushed a kiss across her forehead. "Yes?"

Her hands began a frantic search for his zipper. Sam accommodated her by rolling off to one side. He captured one pert nipple in his mouth as she fumbled with the snap. The relief of the intense pressure of confinement followed the rasp of metal on metal. When her fingertip slipped beneath the waistband of his boxer shorts, Sam tensed and silently begged for control. If she touched him, he knew it would be over too soon.

Capturing her wrist, he brought her hand to his mouth and placed several kisses against her palm. Their eyes met in a long, silent dialogue of desire. He placed her hand against his chest. She immediately began an exploration of the tense muscles at his neck. Balancing on his forearms, Sam's eyes remained fixed on her as he slowly ground himself against her, reveling in the heat emanating from her body. She arched against him, her mouth seeking his. Sam countered her actions but maintained the slow gyration of his hips.

Her movements became more insistent. He felt her feet wrap around his ankles, joining their bodies and enhancing the intimate contact. Her fingers roamed over his biceps, squeezing and massaging the muscles.

He leaned down and kissed her with a thoroughness meant to leave her breathless. It worked. He found her flushed as he watched her take her lower lip between her teeth. He kissed the drop of perspiration between her breasts as he slowly eased off her.

The nightgown came off and he tossed it mindlessly to the floor. Sam stood and removed what was left of his clothing, all the while his eyes remaining on her. The sight of her wide-eyed admiration filled him with arrogant pride as he joined her on the bed.

He lay beside her, his head on his bent arm. He allowed his other hand to rest on her abdomen. The heat of her skin nearly scorched him, and she tried to turn toward him.

"Don't," he said gently as his fingers toyed with the lacy top of her panties.

He could feel the small shivers of anticipation surge through her each time his fingertip slipped beneath the silk. He nuzzled her neck as the exploration continued. He called on all his control as he discovered every delicate inch of her body. Finally, when he could no longer bear the sweet agony, he whisked the panties off and positioned himself between her legs.

Callie closed her eyes and lifted her willing body toward him. Sam remained poised above her, but his lips found hers. The deep, demanding kiss lasted for several mind-shattering minutes. He lifted his head and said, "Look at me. I want to see your eyes when it happens."

Callie complied, and he nearly dissolved when he saw his own searing heat mirrored in her expression. He pushed himself into her with slow, tender movements. He felt her nails dig into his shoulders as his body filled her. Sam gritted his teeth as they fell into the primitive rhythm. He felt her body building toward release as he increased the tempo of their lovemaking. When he at last felt the convulsions of her body around him he allowed himself to savor his own release.

SATISFIED BEYOND BELIEF, Callie lay staring at the ceiling above her. A myriad of emotions coursed through her mind, driving away the certainty she'd felt. How could she have let this happen?

"Is this a guilty silence?" Sam's soft voice floated through the darkening room.

"A little," she admitted. "I don't know what—"

"Don't," he insisted. He gathered her against him, gently stroking her hair as she rested against his chest.

She could feel the even beat of his heart against her cheek as her hand instinctively rested in the thick mat of hair.

"It doesn't matter why we made love."

"Yes it does," she argued, more with herself than with him. "What kind of person seduces a man she barely knows? Especially one on the rebound! At least this time I'm on the pill."

"Really?" Sam asked. She could hear the relief in his tone, and it rankled.

"For my skin," she announced as she rolled away from him and gathered her clothing. She dressed, sitting on the edge of the bed with her back to him. "Let's pretend this didn't happen."

"Okay," Sam said easily.

Too easily, she thought as she said, "I'm going downstairs to get some water."

"I'll get it for you," Sam offered.

"Nope." She turned and made a point of looking only at his face. "The glass of water is subterfuge. It's to give you a chance to get dressed and leave without further discussion."

"Oh," Sam responded.

Callie went downstairs as fast as if the devil himself was chasing her. In a way he was. "What in the world were you thinking?" Callie asked herself as she got down a glass. *Worse still, what must he be thinking?*

Callie cursed softly when she dropped the glass and it broke. It took her a minute to find a dustpan and brush. She swept up the glass and placed it into a full trash can. She pulled the bag from the trash can and opened the back door to put it outside.

Taped to the exterior of the door was an envelope with her name typed in all capital letters. She put the bag of trash down and pulled the envelope off the door.

She read it, then let out a strangled cry.

Chapter Eight

"Let me see it," Sam demanded.

Still shaking, she handed him the note. Sam scanned the page and felt as if someone had sucker punched him in the gut.

"What does that mean?" Callie demanded. "Did the kidnapper contact you?"

Reluctantly Sam nodded, wondering how to explain the note to her without telling her of his suspicions. "I didn't know it was the kidnapper at the time," he offered lamely.

"The note says she warned you that someone would die. Is that true?"

She was looking at him with the hurt of betrayal in her beautiful eyes. Sam simply shrugged.

Placing her hands on her slender hips, Callie glared at him. "Is that why you wanted to send Kevin away? What kind of father gets a threat and leaves his son in harm's way?"

Sam bristled as if she had slapped him. "I was *trying* to get my son out of harm's way, and it cost

Mrs. Lange her life. How do you think that makes me feel?''

"You're an idiot," Callie fumed. "I'm leaving here tonight. Apparently she knows where I am at all times. I won't risk the safety of anyone in this house any longer."

"Whose safety?" Shane asked casually as he came in the back door and hung his jacket on a hook.

"Mrs. Lange was killed because of me," Callie said, her eyes filling with tears. "And it could have been avoided if your brother had told me the truth sooner."

"You told her?" Shane asked in amazement.

Sam glared a warning at his youngest brother. "Yes, I told her all about *the threatening phone call* I received."

Shane nodded with a veiled expression on his face, and then he sighed and started to leave the room. As he walked past Sam he whispered, "I told you this would all come back to bite you on the butt."

Ignoring his brother's comment, Sam squared his shoulders and trapped Callie between the stove and his large frame. "You are *not* going back to your place. It's too dangerous and I won't allow it."

Callie squared her shoulders and met his gaze with fierce eyes. "I don't need your permission, Landry. Get out of my way."

He scowled down at her. "Mrs. Lange was killed by whomever is taunting you. I made love to you. Those two things make this a personal matter to me now. You'll stay here where I know you're safe, until I figure out who is doing this. That is final, Callie."

He watched her cheeks glow to a warm blush. He didn't know whether she was angry about his insistence or angry that they had been intimate. It didn't really matter, he wasn't going to allow her to run straight into a dangerous situation. Not now.

"I don't want to make the kidnapper mad," she explained through clenched teeth. "What if she gets so angry that she hurts Michael?"

Sam averted his gaze. "I can promise you *that* will not happen."

"Really? How?"

He rubbed his face to buy some time. "Well, because. If she loves him enough to send you notes on his progress, she won't want to hurt him."

"From your mouth to God's ear," Callie said. She wrapped her arms around her small body and dropped her head.

Sam could tell by the movements of her shoulders that she was crying. *God, this was getting complicated.*

At a loss for words, Sam gently pulled her into his embrace. He felt her tears against his bare chest. He stroked her hair until silent sobs stopped racking her body.

"It's been a tough day," he said, still holding her. "I'll call down to the bunkhouse and make sure the perimeter of the house is covered at all times. We'll start fresh in the morning on York's reports."

He felt her nod. "What about Kevin?"

"I'll keep him here under watch. I'm sure he'll miss his friends at Little World, but he'll get over it."

"What about Shane?"

Sam gave a humorless little laugh. "Shane can handle anything and anyone."

CALLIE SUCKED IN A deep breath, enjoying the scent of Sam on her pillow. In the light of a new day, it didn't seem so wrong. What was wrong about two people—friends—sharing a one-time, mind-shattering, world-class lapse in judgment? Guessing Sam would pretend it had never happened, Callie practiced that same reaction as she showered and dressed.

When she arrived downstairs, Shane had already gone for the day. Kevin was nowhere to be seen, but she found Sam in the office, poring over the copies of Jim's reports.

"Morning," he said without looking up.

"Good morning. Where is Kevin?"

She heard a soft "Don't tell her where I am!" come from under the desk.

Callie smiled. "I'm going to get some coffee, then I'll come back and help you."

She heard an unhappy grunt from the unseen Kevin, and wondered what it would take to get the child to warm up to her. Melt or die were the options Kevin had suggested thus far.

When she returned with her coffee, she asked, "Is it safe?" in a whisper.

"He went to watch television," Sam said. "Drag a chair around, I've only gotten as far as the initial reports to the police on the day…uh…your son was taken."

Callie dragged a chair around, knowing full well that she could recite the police reports by rote.

"Have you gotten to the part that says 'Mother hysterical, interview later'? As if anyone would be calm learning someone had walked off with their newborn."

"Did the police interview Brittany and David?" Sam asked.

Callie nodded. "They were out of town, but the FBI did get to them, and let me tell you, Brittany was extremely angry at being disturbed on vacation."

Sam appeared shocked. "She was?"

"She called me at the hospital. If I remember correctly, she reminded me that she and David wanted nothing to do with the little bastard, so why would I have sent the authorities to disturb them?"

She saw Sam clench a fist. "That sounds like the Brittany I know. She's the full definition of a bitch. Reminds me of someone else."

"Who?" Callie asked, though she anticipated his response would be his late wife.

"Lynn," Sam admitted, his eyes averted. "I was taken in by her looks and her act. It turned out all she wanted from me was financial stability for her and Kevin."

"Why would she think you wouldn't provide for your son?" Callie asked.

Sam cleared his throat and said, "Who knows? Getting back on track, did the baby have any birthmarks or moles?"

Callie shook her head. "He was perfect." She smiled as one of her favorite memories returned. "I unwrapped him to count toes and fingers." She took in a deep breath. "That seems like a hundred years ago now."

Surprisingly Sam didn't look up, but he did slide his hand over to give hers a reassuring squeeze. That small gesture made her heart sing. Even though she was making a valiant attempt to pretend their intimacy had meant nothing, deep within her, she knew that wasn't true. She'd had a few opportunities with men in the three years since Michael's birth, but she had shunned them all. *So why him?* she wondered.

"Mary was with you when the hospital realized your son had been taken from the nursery?"

"Yes," Callie answered. "I think she went into shock. She barely spoke for weeks after Michael was kidnapped."

"At least that lets her off the hook," Sam opined.

Callie gave him a gentle shove. "I think I would have noticed if my stepmother suddenly had a baby."

"I thought you didn't have contact with your father."

Callie shrugged. "I hoped that learning my son

was kidnapped would earn me some compassion from my father. I was mistaken.''

''Parents can be tough to figure out,'' Sam agreed.

''How do you handle not knowing where either of your parents are?'' she asked.

Sam's head whipped up, his expression hard.

Callie raised her hands and said, ''Sorry. I wasn't trying to pry. I just thought that gave us something in common.''

''I think we created something in common last night,'' Sam said.

''Are we going to have a postmortem now?''

''No.'' Sam's attention returned to the papers. ''I just want you to know that no matter what happens in the future, *that* was real. I don't have a single regret, Callie. I just want us to be clear that it won't happen again.''

Something about his tone sounded ominous. ''So I understand…you enjoyed it, but not enough for a repeat performance?''

She heard him expel a slow breath. ''I've known you less than a week, Callie. I don't want to make the same mistake I made with Lynn.''

''Which was?''

''I jumped into that relationship with my eyes closed. I paid dearly for my mistake.''

''Then why did you stay married?''

''For Kevin's sake.''

''I guess that's a good reason. But if you were having trouble from the beginning, why did you have a child?''

Sam was quiet for a minute, then said, "Don't forget that I didn't ask you about protection beforehand. I guess we can just agree that I'm pretty irresponsible when it comes to sex."

"Didn't you realize that I wouldn't have taken that risk? I've already had one child outside of marriage, I'm not going to do it a second time. Going through a pregnancy and a birth without any support is..." She didn't finish.

Sam met her gaze, his expression unreadable. "Was it hard?"

Callie shrugged. "Being pregnant and alone isn't something I would recommend. But Michael was worth it."

"What would you do if you found out Michael was living with a family who loved him?"

Callie made a derisive sound. "I'd make sure they went to jail."

"What if your son didn't want to go with you? I mean, you would be taking him away from the only parents he's ever known."

Callie bristled. "The kidnapper didn't mind when she took my son. I won't exactly feel sorry for her when she's caught."

"But what about your son? Shouldn't you take into consideration his feelings and best interests?"

"His best interest is to be with his mother." Callie stood, letting out a deep, frustrated breath. "If your goal was to make me angry, Landry, you succeeded. I can't believe you have even an ounce of sympathy for the person or persons who took my baby from me. You're a father. How would you feel if someone took Kevin away from you?"

SAM WAS STILL HOLDING his head in his hands when Shane walked in a half hour later. He closed the door behind him. "What did you do to her? She looks as if she lost her only friend in the world." Shane said. Actually, it was more like an accusation.

Sam looked up. "Why?"

"She's out on the porch, swinging back and forth and staring off into space. She didn't even acknowledge me when I walked past her."

"Are there men around her?"

Shane nodded. "So what gives?"

Self-loathing washed over Sam. "I've complicated this whole mess eight ways to Sunday."

Shane fell into the chair. "Geez, you slept with her!" It was an admonition rather than a question.

"I sure as hell didn't mean for it to happen."

"Then you keep your fly zipped, big bro. It's called self-control."

Sam glared at his brother. "I'd like to see you exercise self-control with a woman like Callie."

"So?" Shane leaned forward. "Have you fallen in love in record time again?"

Sam rubbed his hands over his face. "It wouldn't matter if I did. She'll hate me no matter what the DNA shows."

"Maybe you should come clean with her *before* the test results come back."

Sam shook his head with conviction. "She'll run

out of here in a second, and I won't be able to protect her. If she does that, she'll be putting her life in danger. I can't let that happen."

"Is that because you feel responsible for her? Or because you have feelings for her?"

"I wish I knew," Sam admitted.

"If you want my advice…" Shane began.

"I don't."

"…you'll give it some time. Maybe what you feel for her is lust. Isn't that what happened between you and Lynn? You mistook lust for love. Don't make that mistake twice."

"I doubt I'll have the chance," Sam said. "I have a very strong feeling that Callie won't like me very much when she finds out all of this is a pretext."

Shane rose. "You should have thought of that before you had sex with the lady."

Sam was mulling over his brother's words when Seth came into the office. Like Shane, he closed the door. "Where is Callie?"

"Back porch," Sam answered. "Why?"

Seth reached into his jacket pocket and produced an envelope. "I pulled a few strings at the lab. I have the preliminary results on the DNA test."

Sam's chest tightened as if caught in a vise. "Well? Is Kevin Callie's missing son?"

CALLIE WAS TIRED of feeling angry. She went back inside to help Sam work through the mounds of papers they had gotten from York. Maybe Sam, with his family clout, could finally help her find Michael and end this nightmare.

She opened the door and found Sam and Seth huddled inside. They both looked up at her with guilty expressions.

"What?" Callie demanded, catching sight of the typed note in Sam's hand. "The kidnapper made contact again?" she asked as she grabbed the paper from Sam.

"Wait!" he yelled.

But it was too late. Callie was already reading the report.

Chapter Nine

"You son of a—" Callie reacted with primal fury, slapping Sam across the face. "You bring me into this house knowing that Kevin is my son and—" Her voice broke. Rage, so strong it made her shake, consumed her. "I'm taking him home and calling the FBI." She glared at Seth. "Some law officer you turned out to be."

"Callie!" Sam called out as she ran from the room. "Please!"

He grabbed her arm just as she stepped out into the hallway. "Let me explain," he pleaded.

Callie stared up at him with all the contempt and loathing she felt. She wasn't the least bit deterred by the fear and apology she saw in his dark, panicked eyes. "Explain what? That you're a criminal?"

"It isn't what you think," he insisted.

She tugged at her trapped arm to no avail. "You and some female accomplice stole my son. Was it your wife? Was she the dark-haired woman on the videotape?"

She saw a flicker of pain in his dark gaze but refused to allow it to assuage her anger.

"You have to believe me, I didn't even know Kevin wasn't Lynn's until months after she died and I tried to adopt him. My first thought was that *she* had adopted him."

Callie grunted and again attempted to yank her arm free. "He wasn't *adopted*. He was stolen. You'll go to jail and I hope you rot there!"

"Daddy?" Kevin appeared in the hallway, apparently alerted by Callie's loud voice.

She got down to his level and started to approach him. "Michael?" she began softly.

"Daddy?" Kevin cried out. His little blue eyes grew wide as Callie continued to close in on him. "No!" he yelled as he tried to run past her to Sam.

Callie captured him in her arms. Kevin immediately began crying hysterically, kicking and flailing in her arms. The rejection by her own baby caused Callie to feel as if her insides were being ripped apart.

The harder she hugged him, the more he struggled to be free of her. Callie felt her heart breaking. She hadn't ever really considered what their reunion would be like, but it wasn't this horrible scene.

"Let him go!" Sam commanded.

Callie turned so that the wiggling, screaming child was out of Sam's grasp. "It's okay, honey," she tried to soothe. It didn't work. Kevin was nearly hysterical, so she lowered him to the floor, and he ran to Sam's opened arms.

His sobs calmed to a few hiccups as Sam stroked the boy's hair and whispered to him softly. Callie's eyes met his as she brushed her hair out of her face. She reached out, but stopped short of touching Kevin's little back. Callie wanted to be the one to comfort him. She felt tears stream down her cheeks and watched helplessly as Sam quieted the boy and then took him upstairs.

SAM FOUND CALLIE SOBBING in the hallway when he returned. She looked positively pitiful.

Kneeling down, Sam lifted her by the shoulders and helped her back into the office. Seth was still there.

Once he had Callie in a chair, he asked Seth to leave.

"I've got to notify the FBI," Seth told him, his voice cracking.

Sam nodded his head. "Give me a couple of hours before you call them, please?"

Seth agreed, then left, but not before he stopped to give Callie's shoulder a squeeze.

Sam leaned against the desk, mere inches from her. "I didn't mean for you to be hurt," he said.

Callie lifted her chin. "You brought me into this house." Her eyes implored him for some sort of explanation. "You made love to me knowing that—"

"I didn't *know*," Sam insisted, taking her hands. "That's why I took you to dinner."

"What?" She blinked, not comprehending.

Holding her hands as if they were his lifelines,

Sam explained. "I met and married Lynn in one week. Kevin was three months old at the time. The marriage was a mistake, but I didn't lie to you when I said Lynn and I stayed together for Kevin's sake. I love him and I knew if Lynn and I divorced, I'd never get to see him again."

"Why did she take him?" Callie asked.

"I don't think she did," Sam said.

Callie's eyes filled with censure. "You think by defending her, I won't take my son from you?"

Sam felt the burn of tears at the backs of his eyes. "He's been with me since he was three months old. Lynn's death was hard on him, Callie. What do you think it will do to him if you take me out of his life, too?"

"He's my son," she said.

"I didn't know that until a few moments ago. As I started to explain, I took you to dinner so I could get something with your DNA on it."

"What?"

"The straw from your drink. I had Chance swab Kevin's mouth, and I sent the stuff to the lab."

"Why didn't you tell me?"

Sam closed his eyes to fight back his own tears. "You told me that false hope had almost killed you. I didn't want to—"

"That's crap, Landry," she countered. "You weren't going to tell me, were you?"

"Eventually," he admitted. "But things got crazy. You were being threatened, I was being threatened."

"Did you ever think that none of this would have

happened if you'd simply called the FBI when you found out your wife wasn't Kevin's biological mother?''

"No," he answered honestly. "In *every* way that matters, Kevin is my son."

She shook her head. "In the *only* way that matters, *Michael* is *my* son."

Sam bristled and tears shimmered in his eyes. "He can have us both, you know."

She shook her head. "You may not go to jail, but I don't want you in my son's life. It will only confuse him."

"He's terrified of you, Callie. Or haven't you noticed that?"

Her lips formed a thin, angry line. "Children are resilient. After we've spent some time *alone,* Michael and I will be fine."

"Maybe, but right now, you and *Kevin* can't be alone."

"Watch how long it takes me to pack," Callie retorted, pulling her hands free.

"It's too dangerous," Sam argued as she moved to the door. "Hate me, but don't let that hatred make you do something that could put both your lives in danger. Or do you want to get him killed?"

"How will letting him know that I'm his mother kill him?"

"Whoever is doing this has gotten more violent since you and I met. Kevin may be a part of it, but I think this is personal, Callie. You're the target and anyone—including Kevin—that gets in the way will be killed, just like Mrs. Lange. Is that what you want?''

"Of course not." Callie stopped dead. "I need some time alone with my son. Time where he can't run to you or your brothers. I need this, Sam. I'm not asking you, I'm telling you.''

Sam mustered the courage to form his sentence. "How about a compromise?"

"Compromise?" Callie repeated, one pale eyebrow arched.

"There's a hunting cabin here on the ranch. Kevin likes it there. You two could go there for a couple of days, and I can keep the place protected by my men. Deal?''

Her head dipped to one side. "You wouldn't interfere?''

"No. Not unless you need me.''

"I don't.''

SHE'D GIVEN UP on calling him Michael after their first ten minutes together. The cabin was a small, single-room log cabin much like the one on her family's ranch, only more upscale. This one had insulation, hot and cold running water and very comfortable rustic furniture. The kitchen was better than the one at her firehouse, and the view was to die for. It would have been a perfect place to spend time with a loved one. Except that Kevin didn't love her at the moment.

Sam had packed all of Kevin's favorite toys. Callie retrieved a well-worn stuffed character from a popular children's television program and held it out to Kevin. "Here, honey. I think he wants to tell you a secret."

Kevin's screams began anew, and he ran to the cabin door and continued to scream, kick and pound while calling for his daddy. Callie was at a loss and beginning to feel panic. She found some crayons and a pad and went over to him. "Want to color?"

He stopped screaming and took the crayons. He used them as tiny missiles, throwing them at her one at a time before he started screaming and calling for Sam again. The wailing went on unabated for the better part of two hours. Callie's panic was now mingled with feelings of helplessness and hopelessness. How could she reach him?

The next hour included lunch. Over the sounds of Kevin's unrelenting screams, Callie made some tuna sandwiches, which she was assured were his favorites. She set up the table and spent about five minutes twisting his napkin into a duck. It was her first attempt at origami and she was quite pleased with herself.

Kevin was still by the window, alternately sobbing and calling for Sam. She took the duck over and said, "Mr. Ducky would like to have lunch with you. Is that all right?"

Kevin's tiny hand reached out and ripped Mr. Ducky's head off, then he fell to the floor and threw a complete tantrum. He rolled, he kicked, he turned red.

Callie couldn't stand to see him in such agony for

another minute. So, drenched in sweat and tired of seeing her son so tortured, she reluctantly abandoned the idea.

"Okay, Kevin. I'll take you back to Daddy."

Twenty minutes later she pulled up in front of the ranch house. Sam was dashing down the stairs before she'd cut the engine.

"What happened?" he asked as he opened the back door and took Kevin out of the car seat. His face was a mask of concern.

Dejected, Callie got out of the car and started to unload the bags of food, clothing and toys. "Don't ask," she grumbled.

"Go on inside," Sam said to Kevin before he came to Callie's aid. "You look horrible."

"Thanks to you, my son can't stand to be in the same room with me. Three hours of nonstop screaming brought that point home."

"Oh," Sam said with a tiny hint of satisfaction.

"This doesn't change anything," Callie insisted. "I'm calling a therapist to arrange some sort of counseling for Kevin and me, so that we can get on with our lives."

"Kevin, huh?" Sam said as they climbed the stairs together.

"Apparently he doesn't like his given name any more than he likes me."

Callie and Sam went into the kitchen. They were the only two adults in the house. Callie started to unpack the bag of food, tossing the perishables and placing the other things in plastic wrap. She tried not to make contact with Sam as they maneuvered in the small space. It worked for the most part, until they reached for the same cabinet at the same time. She hated the fact that her traitorous body reacted to the brush of his fingers against the back of her hand. Even worse was the fact that his cologne was annoyingly comforting. *I hate him, right?*

"I know you hate me right now," Sam said.

He was standing behind her, not close enough for their bodies to touch, but close enough for Callie to feel the heat emanating from him.

"What was your first clue?" she retorted smartly.

"Can we be civil, please? For Kevin's sake?"

The feel of his breath against her ear was distracting. "Under the circumstances, you're lucky I haven't done you in with one of those knives over there."

His faint laughter filled the small space between them. "I see you haven't lost your ability to laugh instead of cry."

"I'm trying, Landry."

He placed his hands at her waist and gently turned her to him. "What if we try to work together?"

"I need to break the bond between you and Kevin. I don't see how having you involved will help."

She watched the pain flash in his eyes and actually found herself feeling sorry for him. "I know you love him," she relented. "Maybe once Kevin and I have bonded, you can play a…*small* role in his life."

"I wasn't talking about Kevin," he said. "I was

suggesting we work together to figure out who took your son.''

"Your wife," Callie answered.

"If that's true, then tell me how my dead wife shot Mrs. Lange yesterday? How did she beat you? How did she send notes, months after she died in a car accident?''

Callie shrugged. She'd been so caught up in learning that Kevin was her son that she hadn't fully focused on the details. "Maybe she had an accomplice.''

"That's a possibility," Sam admitted. "Lynn was paying someone a thousand dollars a month while we were married. But after reading those notes you got from the kidnapper, I can promise you, Lynn didn't write them.''

Callie was stunned. "So you're saying that your wife had an accomplice who was blackmailing her, and that accomplice is the person who is trying to kill all of us now?''

"We know it isn't Lynn. If I could see the tape from the hospital that day, I could tell you whether it was Lynn who carried him out.''

"I thought you said she was a strawberry blonde.''

"Wig?" Sam suggested.

"Possibly," Callie agreed. "So, who were her friends? Who could have helped her take Kevin from the hospital?''

Sam took her by the hand. "I'm hoping there will be some indication in York's reports. Something that didn't mean anything to him or to you, but *will* mean something to me.''

"Let's go take another look,'' Callie agreed. She gave his hand a gentle tug and got his full attention. ''I want to find out who took my son so they can be punished, but this doesn't change anything, Sam. He's mine, not yours.''

"We can work all that out later,'' Sam promised. ''We know where Kevin came from and where he ended up. All we need to do is figure out how he got here.''

She was too exhausted from going ten rounds with a screaming three-year-old to counter his suggestion that they could work out Kevin's future later. For the time being she was just thrilled to know that her three-year ordeal was over.

Callie and Sam had been cooped up in the office for almost two hours when Callie reread York's last report. ''What was the name of Kevin's day-care center?''

"Little World,'' Sam answered. ''Why?''

Callie passed Sam the report with its attachments. ''Jim and I decided to try to find my son by checking out day-care centers around the state. Here's the roster from Little World dated a month ago.''

"And?''

"Kevin's name isn't on it.''

Chapter Ten

Sam was sure his excited expression mirrored her own. "Sounds like we've got a lead."

Callie dialed Jim York's number but got no answer. She dialed his pager, but the call still wasn't returned thirty minutes later. Which was precisely when Seth and two FBI agents entered the house.

"Sam, Callie," Seth began, "these are Agents Banks and Sinclair from the Helena office of the FBI.

Callie and Sam greeted them. Agent Banks spoke first. "We'll have to take the little boy into custody, have him checked for—"

"Like hell," Callie exploded. "You are not taking my son anywhere."

"Ma'am," Banks said, clearing his throat nervously, "we need to have the boy examined for possible sex—"

"Finish that sentence and you'll be on your way to a dentist's office," Sam warned. "Callie and I will be glad to cooperate by answering questions, but you'll leave my son out of this."

"Sam's right," Callie added quickly. "*My* son has already been traumatized enough. He doesn't know Sam isn't his father nor does he know I'm his mother. He's only three for God's sake!"

"It's customary practice to—"

"I don't care if the president gave the order," Callie interjected. "He was only a few hours old when he was kidnapped. It isn't as though he can give you a description. You get Sam and me or you get nothing. Your choice."

The agents exchanged quick glances, then informed them that Callie and Sam should be interviewed separately.

"Wrong again," Sam said. He turned and looked directly at Callie before adding, "I don't want there to be any more secrets between Callie and me."

Seth stepped in between Sam and Agent Banks. "Our housekeeper was killed last night. We just got the DNA proof on Kevin this morning. Everyone's a little on edge, so could you cut them some slack?"

Sam hoped the agent said no. Then he could punch the guy and somehow that would feel great.

They relented, and Sam went first, explaining how and where he had met Lynn. Their strained marriage, the thousand-dollar withdrawals, his investigation of Lynn's hysterectomy in Ohio, everything.

He listened as Callie retold the painful story of her baby's abduction, followed by three years of torment from the kidnapper.

"Can we assume that your late wife was the one

who physically removed the child from the hospital nursery?'' Banks asked.

"If you show me the tape,'' Sam said. "I was married to her for nearly three years, I would recognize her walk.''

"We'll have a copy made,'' Banks said. "Or you can come to Helena and review the original.''

"Send the copy.''

Agent Sinclair then said, "I think we should hold a press conference and announce that the child has been recovered.''

"Why?'' Callie asked, her voice tremulous.

Sam placed a protective arm around her. "We're not running a sideshow.''

"We need to draw the kidnapper out,'' Sinclair said. "If we hold the press conference, it is reasonable to believe that another attempt on your lives will be made. I'll need a list of your enemies, Miss Walters, and one from you, Mr. Landry, and I'll post agents on—''

"No way!'' Callie screamed. "First off, I don't have enemies and secondly, I will not permit you to place Kevin or Sam in more danger than they're already in.''

At least she doesn't want me killed, Sam thought. *It's a start.*

"We've done this many times before with mostly positive results,'' Sinclair argued.

"*Mostly* positive?'' Sam repeated somberly. "I don't think I like your odds, pal. You guys do whatever you have to on your end that doesn't include endangering Callie or Kevin. Anything happens to either one of them and I'll—''

"My brother is very protective, as you can see," Seth said. "He also knows better than to threaten a federal agent in the course of an investigation. However, I'll make sure he understands that you don't have the authority to violate their privacy."

Seth left, dragging the agents in tow. Sam and Callie waited for Shane to return to watch over Kevin before they headed back to Jim York's trailer.

The place hadn't improved in the hours since their last visit. Unless you counted the dog, Sam mused. The mutt was no longer tied to the railing of York's trailer.

With Callie close enough behind him for her perfume to be a distraction, Sam climbed the sloped steps and knocked on the flimsy door.

No reply.

Callie stepped to his side and called York's name. Still nothing.

"He ain't there."

Sam turned to find a woman leaning on an uneven bit of fencing that separated her yard from York's. "He isn't?"

The woman frowned and planted her hands on her ample hips. Sam couldn't even guess at her age, but something in her eyes told him that regardless of birthdays, she was an old woman.

"Took off yesterday afternoon. Must be on some big case."

"Why would you say that?" Callie inquired.

The woman shrugged her bony shoulders. "He musta made a dozen trips to the car and back. Seemed like he loaded everything he owned."

"Thanks," Sam said, then he took Callie's hand and started down the steps while the neighbor went back inside her home.

"Sam?" Callie questioned when he abruptly changed directions. "You heard the woman, Jim is off on a case."

"Which is a gift from above," Sam said, careful to keep his voice down. Reaching into his pants pocket, he pulled out his wallet and slipped one of his credit cards from its slot. He slipped it between the frame and the door, lifting and twisting the knob until the door opened.

"We can't do this!" Callie whispered.

"We just did," Sam countered.

The interior of the trailer smelled of coffee and beer, which Sam concluded were probably York's two favorite food groups. He found a switch on the wall and filled the rooms with light. The trailer was decorated in early yard sale and could do with a very thorough cleaning. He glanced back and saw Callie lingering in the doorway. "If you help me, this won't take as long."

"What is 'this'?" she asked, warily.

"We'll know if we find it," Sam said. He went over to a desk with only three legs. The fourth leg was a stack of bricks that almost made it level. The dust outline on the top of the desk told him that a computer had resided on there until quite recently.

"What kind of case would require York to take a desktop computer along? A little on the bulky side," Sam remarked.

"This is weird," he heard Callie say.

He looked over and saw she was holding up an unopened package from the courier service he used at the office. "He seemed reluctant to give these up, then he doesn't take the time to file them before he leaves. After someone decided to beat you to a pulp and steal your copies."

"I don't know why," Callie said, her tone a tad less supportive of her P.I.

"Maybe the kidnapper just wanted to take the only things you had of your son," Sam mused. "Which still tells me this is personal to you."

"I'll go see what's in the bedroom," she said. "I hope I don't catch anything in there. This place gives new meaning to the expression hellhole."

Sam opened every drawer in the living room and kitchen area. He found nothing except filth. He noticed a pad on the chipped counter. The top sheet had been torn off haphazardly. Like maybe York had been in a hurry.

"I didn't find anything," Callie said when she rejoined him.

Sam watched her walk down the narrow hallway. Her hips swayed as she moved, causing her ankle-length skirt to rustle slightly. He knew he shouldn't be noticing such things, but for some reason York's secretive behavior suddenly wasn't as important as watching Callie move. She had pulled some of her pale hair into a clip at the back of her head. Several strands were left free, providing a feathery frame for her stunning face. He loved the way she moved. *Loved? Where did that come from?*

"Why are you staring at me?" Callie asked. Her small hand immediately went to the bandage Sam no longer even noticed.

No more secrets, he had vowed, so he simply answered, "Because you're very beautiful."

He saw color rise on her cheeks just below the darkened circles left over from the beating she had suffered. Just thinking about that made his blood boil.

"Don't do this, Sam."

"Do what?" he asked quietly as she neared him and stopped. She was close enough that all he'd have to do was reach out and she would be in his arms.

"Start this…this…*anything!*"

"I was merely making an observation and answering you honestly. I promised myself that I wouldn't lie to you ever again."

"I'm a mess right now, Sam. I'm giddy, finally knowing where my son is, but I'm heartbroken at his reaction to me." She brushed her hair off her forehead. "Oh Gosh!" she suddenly shouted. "Between my unproductive hours at the cabin with Kevin and those stupid FBI people, I haven't called Mary!"

"Here," Sam said, handing her his cell phone.

A few minutes later Callie announced, "Mary wants to meet Kevin."

Sam felt his brow furrow. "What about your fa-

ther?'' He saw the flash of uncertainty in her eyes.
''Maybe you should call back and arrange for Mary
to come out to the ranch.''

Callie vehemently shook her head. ''Like it or not,
my father is going to meet his grandson. Maybe once
he gets a look at how beautiful Kevin is, he'll forget
all his hostility.''

Sam wasn't sure, but he also didn't want to alien-
ate Callie in any way. It was important for him to
regain her trust. He wanted her to look at him the
way she had the night they'd made love. He shook
his head, rattled by the unexpected train of thought.
He wanted Kevin, not Callie, right? He didn't want
to repeat his earlier mistake of moving too fast too
soon.

''You're frowning,'' Callie commented as he held
open the door of the Jag for her.

Sam forced a half smile. ''Sorry, I was just thinking about something.''

She lifted compassionate eyes to him. Something
he hadn't expected. ''I'm sure the thought of losing
Kevin is hard, but as I said, once I've had an opportunity to explain to him that I'm his mother and
we've had some counseling, I will allow you some
sort of limited access.''

Sam swallowed the lump of emotion in his throat.
''It doesn't have to be like that.''

''Yes,'' Callie said softly, ''it does.''

THEY ARRIVED BACK at the ranch and found Kevin
asleep on the sofa. Callie remained in the doorway

as he went over and stroked the little boy's head. The mere thought of losing Kevin made him feel as if someone was reaching inside his chest and slowly tearing his heart out.

Kevin's blue eyes fluttered half-open. Seeing Sam, he smiled and said, "Hi, Daddy," before he drifted back to sleep.

How would he cope with never hearing Kevin call him Daddy again? Never being awakened by Kevin prying his eyes open? He continued to stroke the boy's cheek. "He likes his juice in a coffee cup. He isn't big on sledding, but he loves to build snowmen. Last summer he learned to doggie paddle in the pool, so next year he should be ready for swimming lessons."

Sam turned and saw tears spilling down Callie's cheeks.

"I'll remember those things," she promised. "How long do you think he'll nap?"

"Another hour or so," Sam said. "He usually crashes from three to five."

She nodded and left the room. Sam stayed for several more minutes. It was his turn to cry in silence.

Shane appeared at the door and motioned to Sam. Sam wiped the tears on his shirtsleeve before joining his brother in the hallway. Shane pulled him into the office, then closed the door. He deposited Sam in a chair, then stood over him like a concerned parent about to question an errant child.

"You didn't shed a tear when the folks took off."

"This is different," Sam said, annoyed that his

voice still cracked with emotion. "Wait until you have a child, then you'll understand."

"There's no way you can arrange something with Callie?" Shane probed.

Sam shook his head, a little amazed by Shane's outward display of concern and affection. "The best she's offering is 'limited contact' after she puts Kevin into therapy for God knows how long."

"So why hasn't she taken the kid and bolted?"

Sam didn't have a concrete answer, so he guessed at her reasons. "I understand Kevin was a terror when she took him to the cabin. She's going to hang out here until she can explain things to Kevin."

Shane whistled. "The kid isn't going to understand you're not his real father. That boy worships you."

"I'm open to ideas on ways to change her mind."

Shane picked a strange moment to smile, but nonetheless he did. "I have a feeling you'll figure something out."

Sam didn't answer. He didn't have the first clue what he was going to do about losing Callie. *Kevin!* his brain screamed. He didn't have a clue what to do about losing Kevin.

"I spoke to Mrs. Lange's sister," Shane was saying just as Sam returned from his conflicted thought. "The funeral is set for day after tomorrow. Cade said he'd fly us all over to Hardin and back."

"Good," Sam said, saddened by the reminder. "Is Barbara going?"

Shane nodded. "You taking the kid?"

It was Sam's turn to nod. "He's too young, but I don't think he'll be thrilled at the idea of staying here with Callie. And I'm not sure I want to give Callie the opportunity to take off with him."

"That's probably a smart idea. Since they still haven't found the creep who beat her, you've got to make her understand that she's safer here where the men can keep an eye on her. But I think I have a solution for you."

Sam lifted his head. "I can't bypass paying my respects," he said. "I need to tell her I'm sorry. I never thought the kidnapper would go after her."

"We all know that," Shane said. "My solution is Taylor Reese."

"Who's he?"

"She," Shane corrected. "She's a part-time student at Montana West University. A friend of a friend told her about Mrs. Lange. She called this morning to see if we'd be interested in hiring her."

"Did Seth check her out?"

"No criminal record, no warrants, not even so much as a traffic ticket. And—" Shane's smile widened "—a voice that makes you weak in the knees."

Sam rolled his eyes. "Maybe it would be better if we found someone old and gnarled. You came back to take over the duties on the ranch. Those duties don't include lusting after the housekeeper."

"Sorry if I offended thee, Saint Sam. But she's worked in two nursery schools as an aide, and I called them both—glowing reviews. And she was completely cool when I told her she might have to watch Kevin every now and then.''

"Assuming he's here,'' Sam lamented. ''I wish I had never tried to adopt him.'' He rubbed his face in his palms and whispered, ''I'd love to go back a week and do things differently.''

Shane patted his shoulder. ''Then you wouldn't have met Callie.''

"But I wouldn't be losing my son.''

"Lemme ask you a question, bro.''

"Shoot.''

"Pretend for a minute that there was no Kevin.''

"I don't think I can do that.''

"Try,'' Shane insisted. ''What if you'd met Callie on the street?''

"Your point?''

Shane rolled his eyes. ''Callie is a beautiful woman. She's your dream woman.''

"Says who?''

"You,'' Shane replied.

"How so?''

"I know you, Sam. If you didn't feel something for her, you never would have made love to her.''

Sam closed his eyes and relived the glorious memory of having her beneath him. He remembered every tiny detail. The way her warm skin flushed and glowed. How her eyes turned darker—more blue— in the heat of passion. Most of all he remembered how incredible it had felt to be inside of her. It was as though they were made for each other. Intimacy had never been like that for him. With Callie, it wasn't just physical, it was—primal. It was right.

What if Shane was on the money? What if he had met Callie under different circumstances? Even though they'd only been together a short time, would she love him instead of hating him?

Callie came in as Shane went out. ''You look horrible,'' she remarked. ''Has something else happened?''

Sam met her gaze and said, ''Yeah.''

Alarmed, Callie rushed to him and asked, ''What?''

He reached out and loosely captured her head, their eyes locked. ''I know you probably won't believe this, but I think I'm falling in love with you.''

Chapter Eleven

She gaped at him for a second, then anger caught fire in her eyes. "Is that what you and Shane were doing in here? Thinking up some excuse to keep me around?"

"No."

"Right," she huffed. "You don't love *me*, Sam. You love Kevin."

"What if I do love you?" he asked sincerely. "I have all the symptoms."

"Like what?"

"I watch you when you aren't looking. I think of you constantly. I feel physically ill at the thought that you will soon be walking out of my life."

Callie blinked as if he'd just explained some complicated scientific theory. Pulling her hand away, she shoved her hair back, and he noticed a slight tremor in her hand. Sam stood and walked to her.

Her perfume scented the air between them. Sam wasn't sure what his next move should be. He was so used to giving orders that he didn't quite know

how to go about convincing Callie to at least consider the possibility that he had feelings for her sep-
arate from his feelings for Kevin. No words came to
him, so he chanced taking action instead.

She flinched slightly when he reached for her and
took her into his arms. Sam held perfectly still, torn
between physical need and emotional greed. Since
she didn't push out of his arms, Sam concluded that
she wasn't completely averse to the idea.

He held her face in his palms, tilting her head
slightly so that he could see her. Happiness filled him
when he noted that her eyes were turning darker.
Nearly the same color as when they had made love.

"This isn't about Kevin," he assured her. "This
is about you and me."

He dipped his head and brushed his lips against
hers. There was no reaction. Sam kissed her more
deeply, pulling her closer as he did. After a few seconds Callie seemed to relax in his arms, until she
was a willing participant in the kiss. His entire body
was hot and molten after she drew his tongue into
her mouth. Sam allowed his hands to move from her
face, down her sides to her waist. He loved feeling
her shiver as his fingers massaged her waist and hips.
Sam actually felt his head swimming. His brain
seemed unable to process anything beyond the incredible feel of her body against his.

"Daddy!"

Callie pulled away from him after hearing Kevin
yell. Sam made a point of keeping one hand around

her waist as he turned his attention to the approaching Kevin.

"What is it, pal?"

Kevin's expression was confusion mixed with concern. "I want a drink."

"I'll get it for you," Callie offered, her voice unsteady.

"No! Daddy!"

Sam knelt and placed his hands on Kevin's little shoulders. "Callie is our friend, Kevin. I won't permit you to keep yelling at her, understand?"

Kevin stuck his quivering lower lip out. "She isn't my friend. She made Mrs. Lange go away."

"No," Sam insisted. "Mrs. Lange is in heaven, just like…Mommy."

"Excuse me," Callie said as she brushed past them. Sam could hear her footfalls as she climbed the stairs in a hurry.

"Why did she run away?" Kevin asked.

Sam stroked his chin and tried to think of a way to explain things to a three-year-old. "Come sit on my lap, pal. We need to have a man-to-man."

That made Kevin smile. He waited for Sam to sit, then happily crawled up into his lap. "You know your cousin Jess?"

Kevin nodded, his eyes wide as saucers. "Is she coming to play with me?"

"Soon," Sam assured him. He sucked in a breath, knowing he was doing the right thing, even though it threatened to rip his gut out. "You know how Jess has two moms?"

"One died and Aunt Barbara took her place," Kevin repeated. "Aunt Barbara is Jess's mom now."

"Right," Sam said, tweaking the boy's nose. "Well, Callie is *your* other mother."

"But I don't like her. Jess likes Aunt Barbara. I don't want an other mother. Uncle Shane can be my other mother."

Sam chuckled. "It doesn't work that way, pal. So you need to give Callie a chance, okay?"

"'Kay," Kevin said without much enthusiasm. "How long does she have to be my other mother?"

Sam hugged Kevin tightly. "Forever."

"Just like you'll be my daddy forever?"

Sam kissed the boy's head and felt the sting of tears at the back of his eyes. "I hope so, pal. You'll always be my son, no matter what happens. Remember that."

SAM TOOK KEVIN up to his room and dressed him in one of his better outfits. Kevin groused and grumbled as Sam explained that they were going to visit some friends of Callie's.

"Why do I have to come, too?"

"Because it's important to Callie. So we both have to go and be on our best behavior." Satisfied that Kevin looked his best, Sam stood up and offered his hand. "Ready?"

"Can I have a treat if I'm good?"

"Absolutely," Sam promised as he guided Kevin from his room.

When they joined Callie in the foyer, it was ap-

parent to Sam that she'd been crying. Her smile
didn't reach her eyes. "Maybe we should do this
another day," she suggested.

"We're all set," Sam said. "Right, Kevin?"

"I get a treat if I behave."

"So Sam...your dad...bribed you?"

Kevin lingered half-hidden behind Sam's thigh. "I
have to be nice because you're my other mother."

Sam thought Callie would explode from sheer joy.
Tears welled in her wide eyes as she knelt to Kevin's
height. "Then would you give your mother a hug?"

"No!" Kevin said firmly. "Jess doesn't have to
hug her aunt Barbara!"

Sam gave Callie an apologetic look. "I'll explain
later."

When she smiled up at him this time, it reached
her eyes. "Thank you for trying. It really means the
world to me."

Reaching out, Sam took Callie's hand and Kevin's
and led them down to a four-by-four owned by one
of the hands. With his men on the lookout, he was
certain no one could be near enough to see them get
in the car. He didn't want to announce their comings
and goings to anyone watching outside the property.

There was something about having Callie and
Kevin with him that felt right. It was as if the three
of them belonged together. All he had to do was
convince Callie of that fact.

The Walters ranch was to the northeast of Helena.
As was their practice, Kevin was strapped into his
car seat with his junior tape player and headphones.

Listening to sing-along tapes seemed to keep him happy on long drives.

"How did you come up with the idea of other mothers?" Callie asked.

Sam shrugged. "My cousin Cade remarried a few months ago. Cade had a daughter with his first wife. I tried to tell Kevin that you were going to be his new mommy just like Barbara was Jess's new mommy. Obviously it wasn't a very good analogy, since Jess is sixteen and shares her time between Cade and Barbara and Cade's former in-laws. Not a traditional family model. I should have tried another tack."

"We can ask the counselor, but until then we'll just have to try to make him understand who I am."

"Lynn was a lousy wife, but she did love Kevin."

"Good," Callie said. "Not the part about being a bad wife. But I'm glad she showed my son love and affection. Why was she a bad wife?"

Sam shrugged. "Maybe I'm being too harsh. I wasn't a great husband, either, I suppose. I wanted things to work, but it didn't matter. Lynn was in love with my bank account, and I was in love with her— *your* son. I made the decision to marry her after a week of picnics and playing with Kevin. I was enthralled with him from the moment I laid eyes on him. I guess he just brought out all my pent-up paternal instincts. Even after Lynn died, Kevin's been surrounded by love and affection. All my brothers adore him."

"I do understand that," Callie said as she touched

her fingertips to his arm. "Which is why I'm willing to overlook what happened in the office. I know you're desperate and you'll do anything to keep Kevin but—"

"My kissing you had nothing to do with Kevin," Sam insisted. "The honest truth is, I'm not sure what true love is. I thought I did when I married Lynn, but I was wrong. I only know that when I'm with you, I feel…complete."

"You shouldn't say things like that. You're only complicating an already-complicated situation."

Sam took her hand, brought it to his lips and kissed her palm. Even using his limited peripheral vision, he saw the effect the kiss had on Callie. "I know you think I've confused my feelings for you with my feelings for Kevin. But you're wrong. I just hope you figure that out before you ruin our family."

"We aren't a family, Sam."

"We could be."

"No, we couldn't," she said with a tinge of sadness in her voice. "You're asking me to overlook the fact that you lied to me."

"I didn't lie!" he insisted in a heated whisper, mindful of Kevin. "I didn't know for sure that Kevin was your missing son until the DNA report. It could just as easily have come back with a different result, which, according to you, could have pushed you over the edge," he argued. "Try to understand that I was damned if I did and damned if I didn't."

"I'll try, if you'll try to remember that my first

concern right now is building a relationship with my son.''

''By yanking him away from the family he loves?'' Sam countered. ''How do you think that will affect him? You've been there, Callie. What did it feel like when your father pushed you away? And you were an adult. Kevin's just a little boy who has already been through the loss of the woman he thinks is his mother. He's witnessed the murder of our housekeeper, whom he adored. At this point I'd be very happy if you would just agree to stay at the ranch and hire your damned counselor. I insist on Kevin's feelings being the barometer for when you take him from me.''

''The longer we stay at the ranch, the harder it will be for me to be a part of Kevin's life.''

''What if we get professional advice?''

''Whose?''

''You pick,'' he said. ''We'll find someone who knows about children and trauma and see what they have to say about the situation. This is new ground for all of us, Callie, and I just don't want Kevin traumatized.''

''I don't, either,'' she insisted. ''Fine. I'll find a therapist and do this *if* you agree to abide by whatever she says.''

''She?''

''I happen to like female doctors. I think they are far more compassionate.''

''Fine,'' Sam agreed. His frustration began to subside. ''I don't mean to be difficult with you.''

"You aren't," she said. "I really do understand how you must feel."

"If you understand so much, how come you won't even consider the possibility that I'm telling the truth about my feelings for you?"

"By your own admission you don't even know what love is."

"And you're an expert?" he asked.

"Yes. I loved Kevin's father. Even though I now know that he never loved me, I can't hate him."

"Why not?"

"Because he gave me Kevin."

"That's virtually the same reason I couldn't end it with Lynn," Sam admitted. "She gave me Kevin."

"Well, gee, put that in the sick coincidence file."

Sam chuckled. "I guess it is a little on the strange side."

"No, strange is what you are about to experience. Take the next left."

"Nervous?" he asked as they approached the house.

"Not really. Unless you count the knot in my gut as a sign of nervousness. If I know my father, he'll be waiting on the steps with his shotgun."

Sam brushed his knuckles across her cheek. "I'm here for you. Just give me a signal if it gets too rough, and we're all out of here."

"Thanks," she answered.

Sam parked at the midpoint of a horseshoe-shaped drive. Like many ranchers Mason Walters was suffering hard times. At least, that was Sam's impression as he looked at a roof that needed fixing and a crooked fence line down by the stables.

A woman came rushing from the house just as he cut the engine. She was short and carried a few extra pounds, and she had a pretty face. She was rubbing her hands excitedly as she reached the car.

"Oh, my," was all she managed to say before tears spilled over her cheeks.

"Best behavior," Sam reminded Kevin. Then he got out of the car to get Kevin from his car seat.

"Michael, you're so adorable come to Gran—"

"Mary," Callie interrupted. "His name is Kevin now, and he doesn't understand all the facts."

Mary looked perplexed as she patted the pile of lacquered white hair that rose about six inches above her scalp. "I don't understand. I thought—"

"I'll explain later. For now, just follow my lead."

Sam carried Kevin over to where the two women stood. "Kevin, this is Mary."

Kevin held out a tiny hand. "How do I do?" he said.

"Precious," Mary exclaimed, tearing up again. "You are the spitting image of—um—a-an angel."

"Kitty!" Kevin exclaimed with glee as he pointed to a gray cat weaving in and out of Mary's legs.

"That's Garbo," Mary told him. "She's a mama cat. Would you like to come inside and see her babies?"

"Yes!" Kevin answered as he tried to wriggle out of Sam's hold. "Can I have one? I *really* need a kitty."

"We'll see," Sam said, shifting Kevin to offer his hand. "Sam Landry, Mrs. Walters."

She took his hand but didn't meet his gaze. Apparently he wasn't the only one feeling awkward.

"Please come inside."

"Is he here?" Callie asked.

Sam watched Mary's apologetic expression as she said, "No, honey. I told him you were coming with the baby, and he refused to stay. I tried."

"I know you did," Callie said as she hugged Mary. "Too bad my father can't follow your lead. No matter what David does, you've always supported him."

Sam was confused. Was "David" David Leary, Kevin's father? What was his connection to Mary?

"I'm sorry," Mary said. "You know I didn't approve of what he did."

"I know," Callie agreed. "So let's go meet those kitties."

The interior of the house was warm, welcoming and very casual. The furniture hadn't been updated in a few decades, but Sam could tell Mary had added handmade touches where possible.

She led them into the dining room and apologized for the sewing machine that was on the table. Kevin didn't focus on anything besides finding the kittens. He gladly went with Mary into the small kitchen adjoining the dining room. There was a box in the far corner, and Kevin refused to take off his coat in favor of holding one of the kittens.

"Gentle," Sam warned.

Kevin cradled the tiny ball of fur against him. It made small mewling sounds, then curled up against Kevin's chest. "I'll name you Red. My favorite Power Ranger is red."

Mary brought out a pot of coffee, then a tray of freshly baked cookies. Kevin passed on the cookies as he exchanged one small kitten for another, which he named Red Number Two.

"Is that from the beating?" Mary asked as she inspected Callie's black eyes and peeked under the bandage. "Have they caught the monster who did this?"

"Not yet," Callie said. "Which reminds me, I have to take a horse pill."

"Do you want some water?" Mary asked.

Callie looked over at Sam and grinned. He knew she was remembering their conversation on the same subject. "Callie is convinced that regardless of the directions printed on the bottle, coffee is all she needs."

"She always has had a mind of her own," Mary commented with genuine affection. "Gets that from her father. They are both as stubborn as mules."

"I've noticed," Sam commented. It earned him an elbow in the ribs from Callie.

"So what do the police think?" Mary asked, obviously deeply concerned.

"The threats are probably from the kidnapper or her accomplice," Sam supplied.

Mary's face went a little pale. "How do they know there's an accomplice?"

Kevin was introducing himself to Red Number Four as Sam quietly explained about his late wife, the withdrawals, the letters, the murder of Mrs. Lange and the sudden disappearance of Jim York. "Callie said you found Jim York for her, is that true?"

Mary fidgeted and said, "Yes. I've known Jim since high school. When Callie said she wanted an investigator, I told her about him."

"Do you have any idea where he might have gone?" Callie asked. "I really need to talk to him about one of his reports."

"Is there a problem?" Mary asked on a rush of breath. In fact, she seemed so genuinely upset that Sam felt pretty certain she wasn't capable of shooting Mrs. Lange or beating Callie to a pulp.

"We just need to check out an error we found. It's probably nothing."

"Can I help?" Mary asked. "I can at least make some calls to mutual friends Jim and I share. Maybe someone knows where he's off to."

"Thanks." Callie covered the older woman's hand with her own. "You've helped me from day one, Mary. I don't know how I would have gotten through the past three years without your love and support. At least you never blamed me for the affair or getting pregnant, unlike my father."

Mary seemed uncomfortable with the attention. "Let's get that boy over here so I can take a good look at him."

Sam got Kevin, promising him he could go back

to naming all the kittens as soon as he had a cookie with Mary.

Mary was a natural grandmother, he thought as he watched her coax Kevin into sitting on her lap. Sam also noticed that Callie looked rather envious.

"He's a sucker for cookies," he whispered.

"Then I'll be using your kitchen a lot. I should have figured the way to a man's heart, even a three-year-old man, was through his stomach."

"Did you grow up in this house?" Sam asked.

"Yep." Callie stood and took Sam by the hand. "I'll give you the grand tour. Is that okay, Mary?"

"This is your home, Callie. You don't have to ask."

"Since my father is outside somewhere, you'll have to settle for a description of the spread. There's a stable and three barns out back. It isn't the Lucky 7, but Dad owns about three thousand acres. Beef cattle," she said as they entered the living room. "There's a hunting cabin in the northwest corner. As for the house, this is the living room. It hasn't changed much over the years."

Sam was drawn to a collection of photographs on one of the end tables. He recognized the woman in the wedding photo as well as in a casual shot. "That's Brittany," Sam said, surprised.

"Yep. She made a beautiful bride. The other picture is from a homecoming game at her college."

"Which one?" Sam asked.

"Miami, I think," Callie said.

"Why would your father and stepmother keep

photographs of Brittany Johnson? Wasn't she the woman David was cheating on when you got pregnant?''

"I want you out of my house!''

Sam and Callie turned at the same time to face the gruff male voice.

"You're looking well, Daddy," Callie said, without so much as a waver in her tone.

"You're a sinner and I won't have a sinner under my roof,'' Mason Walters announced.

"I found my son, I thought—''

"You thought wrong,'' Mason interrupted tersely. "That child is the work of Satan.''

Sam stepped forward, only to have Callie grab his arm.

"Forget it,'' Callie said. "We'll leave.''

"Good.'' Mason sneered. "I can't stand the sight of you.''

"You're a sorry excuse for a father,'' Sam snapped. "How can you be so cruel to your child?''

"I guess she hasn't told you the whole truth, eh?''

"Let's go, Sam,'' Callie fairly pleaded.

"Tell him,'' Mason taunted. "Tell your fancy new boyfriend that you got pregnant by your own brother!''

Chapter Twelve

It wasn't until they had returned to the ranch, had dinner and put Kevin to bed that Callie was able to explain her father's hateful words.

"I don't have a brother," Callie explained. "When my father remarried, I was fourteen. Mary had a son from her first marriage, but he was ten years older than I was, and we never even lived in the same house."

"David Leary is Mary's son?" Sam asked. "That explains the picture of Brittany in your father's house."

"I knew my father thought of David as his own son, so I kept our relationship a secret from everyone."

"Until you got pregnant?"

"Actually, David told me about Brittany before that. We had broken up and then I found out I was pregnant. I was just young and stupid enough to think he'd come back to me if he knew I was carrying his child."

"No fairy-tale ending?" Sam asked.

"Hardly. David told Mary, Mary told my father and Daddy has basically refused to so much as speak to me since then. Just consider us the poster children for the dysfunctional family."

Sam stood, took her hands and gently pulled her to her feet. "I'm sorry you were hurt."

Callie knew she should just thank him and be on her merry way to bed. However, what she wanted overruled the should. It felt perfectly wonderful to be held against his big, strong body. Being in Sam's arms was like coming home. It felt right even if it was very wrong.

"No necking in the kitchen," Shane quipped as he came in, his long hair damp from the shower. "The sexy-voiced Taylor Reese is coming over this evening."

Sam turned Callie in his arms so that her back was pressed against him. His hands entwined with hers, resting comfortably against her abdomen. They probably looked like the perfect couple, Callie thought. This was getting too confusing. If she had half a brain, she'd take Kevin back to her place and put as much distance between them as possible.

Obviously she didn't have half a brain. She relaxed, allowing her head to rest against Sam's chest. She could feel the even rhythm of his breathing. Smell the fresh scent of his cologne. She seemed aware of everything. The smoothness of his silk shirt in contrast to the rough denim jeans. Her interest didn't stop there. She felt the slight pressure at her back as his body responded to the intimate contact. Thank God Shane was there or she'd probably make another major mistake.

"We aren't necking," Sam grumbled. "We *could* have been, until you interrupted."

Shane's smile was almost boyish and definitely devilish. "Think of me as your conscience, big bro. I'm just looking out for the lady's honor. I can't have you ravaging her at your whim."

"Thank you, kind sir," Callie teased as she stepped away from Sam.

"Don't thank me," Shane teased back. "I'm hoping you'll tire of the old man and set your sights on his more attractive younger brother."

"In your dreams," Sam scoffed. "Why would she want a boy when she can have a man?"

"I think I'll let you two finish this silly pissing match without me." She hastily exited the room. "I'll go freshen up. I wouldn't want to miss meeting the sexy-voiced Taylor Reese."

SAM HAD TO ADMIT his brother had been right about Taylor's voice. For such a tiny wisp of a girl, she had a deep, raspy voice that seemed to be an invitation to share her bed even when she was discussing her job responsibilities. Somehow the woman made vacuuming sound like foreplay. And Shane was hanging on every word. If Callie hadn't appeared at that moment, Sam was sure his brother would have started drooling.

"I'm Callie," she said, extending her hand.

Though Taylor would be considered very pretty in any circle, to Sam she paled badly in comparison to Callie. Callie had the smarts and the body of a woman. Taylor wasn't quite up to that league yet.

"Which one of these two do you belong to?" Taylor asked.

"Neither."

"Me," Sam corrected. "She just won't admit it yet."

"Don't mind him," Callie dismissed. "I think he was dropped on his head as a small child. He suffers from delusions now."

"I don't," Shane piped up. "I'm perfect in every way, want to see?"

Taylor gave Shane a rather haughty going-over before answering, "No, not particularly. Unless you'd like me to tend that bruise by your throat. What happened?"

"He's into self-abusive behavior," Sam assured her. "He inflicts injuries on himself to get attention. He's done it since childhood."

"It looks bad," Taylor commented as she went straight over to Shane and began unbuttoning his shirt. Sam and Callie held in their laughter as Taylor examined every inch of Shane's torso. Shane was gnawing on his lower lip, but Taylor seemed completely unfazed by the incident. "You'll live," she announced. "What kind of wax do you use on these floors?"

Callie and Sam could barely contain their amusement. If Callie hadn't been squeezing his hand, he probably would have doubled over in laughter. If Shane had thought he was going to make Taylor more than just a housekeeper, she had beautifully quashed any such notion.

"What about the little boy? Kevin?"

Sam watched Callie's expression grow somber. "It's my understanding that Shane explained to you that we've had some trouble."

She nodded. "I'm sorry about your former house-keeper."

"For now, you'll have to give a list of anything you need to one of the hands. They will do all the shopping and errands. Shane and I will arrange something for getting you back and forth to school."

"I'm pretty self-reliant, Mr. Landry."

"Sam," he corrected. "I'm sure you are, but we aren't taking any chances. I've got an appointment with Kevin's day care tomorrow. We're going to see if there's a way to let him play with his friends without putting anyone in danger."

"You folks seemed to have covered every angle," Taylor commented. "I'm a great shot if you want to leave a handgun in the house."

"No," Callie and Sam said in unison.

Callie regrouped first and explained, "I don't want any guns, even unloaded ones, where Kevin could get his hands on them."

"All of the weapons are under lock and key at the bunkhouse," Sam said. "You see or hear anything suspicious, you call down there immediately."

"Sure," Taylor agreed easily.

"Are you certain you want this job?" Sam asked. "We can fend for ourselves until this…er…*situation* is handled."

"I spent two years teaching in Africa. I lived through tribal conflicts that were nothing in comparison to the violence I lived through at the Big Sky Home for Girls."

"The what?" Sam asked.

"My father abandoned me ten years ago. They stuck me in a state home until I reached eighteen. Then a stint with the Peace Corps and now I'm working on a degree in psychology at Montana West."

"Are any of your faculty practicing therapists?" Callie inquired.

"Most of them maintain a private practice."

"Any of them specialize in treating trauma patients or children in crisis?"

Taylor smiled. "Molly Jameson. She's great. She's published four books on the effects of sudden trauma on children and adults. She also counsels couples going through trauma, like losing a child, that sort of stuff."

"May I have her phone number?" Callie asked.

Taylor dug into a backpack and pulled out a business card. "I guess having some creep hunting you qualifies as trauma." She handed Callie the card. "Tell her I sent you, it might help you get an appointment a little quicker."

"Thanks."

"Where do you want me to get started?" Taylor asked.

"How about on me?" Shane suggested. "I've got a really sore shoulder. One of the bulls rammed me into some fencing earlier and I need—"

"A hot bath," Taylor advised him. "I've got a bag out in the car. Just show me to my room and I'll get settled. Any requests for breakfast?"

Shane opened his mouth, but a pointed look from Taylor warned him off.

"Kevin likes waffles," Sam said.

"With or without fruit?"

"Without. He also drinks juice out of a coffee mug."

"Got it," she said. "I'll get settled and see everyone at breakfast. What time?"

"Between five-thirty and six," Shane said, a tad subdued by the new housekeeper.

"See you all tomorrow morning, then. Just point me in the right direction."

Shane did the honors, and Sam was surprised when he turned and saw Callie on the verge of tears. "What?" he said, wiping them away with his thumbs. "What's wrong, Callie? If you don't like her—"

"It isn't her. It's me."

"You haven't done anything."

"That's the point. When it comes to Kevin, I haven't done anything. I don't know his favorite foods or his favorite toys. Until today, I didn't know he liked the red Power Ranger the best. There's so much about him that I don't know and I'm his *mother*."

"I'll help you, Callie. You know that."

She lifted her head and met his dark gaze. "I'm not sure I know anything anymore."

Sam swallowed his smile. "At least the kidnapper or her accomplice has been quiet."

"Is that good or bad?" Callie asked.

"Bad," Shane said as he hurried back into the room waving an envelope. "It's got Callie's name typed on it, just like the other one."

"How the hell is he getting to the back door unseen?" Sam demanded.

"I'll ask the men," Shane promised. "Obviously someone isn't doing his job, and whoever it is won't have one when I'm finished."

Sam ripped open the letter and found it brief but disturbing. Aloud, he read, "You found the kid. Now stop looking for me, or I'll take him again, and this time it won't be to a good family, it will be to his grave."

He wrapped Callie in his arms and cursed as she began to shake with silent sobs.

SAM AND CALLIE TOOK yet another car into town the next morning. Sam would have preferred to do this stuff alone, but Callie was insistent. Probably because she didn't want to sit around and watch Kevin fawn over Taylor. The boy had taken to the young woman quickly, thanks in part to the fact that she made faces out of whipped cream on his waffles.

Little World day-care center was at the end of Main Street in the heart of town. It was two doors down from Chance's office, which had been a major plus. Often Chance would spend his lunchtime with Kevin.

"This is adorable," Callie said when he parked in front of the day-care center. "It looks like a playhouse."

"It's a great place," Sam said with genuine admiration. "Wait until you get a look at the inside."

He was pleased that Callie liked the place. Somehow it mattered to him that she approve of the things he'd done for Kevin.

"Hello, Mr. Landry." A thin woman with long, brown hair greeted him. She wiped her hands on a paint smock before shaking his hand.

"Julie, this is Callie Walters. I was hoping Mrs. Harrington was in so that I could speak to her."

"She's upstairs, go on up," Julie said brightly.

Their progress was delayed when Callie was drawn to a little girl of about four. Sam recalled her name was something trendy, the name of a state or a city. Madison, Dakota, one of those.

Leaving Julie for a moment, he moved in to watch Callie offer painting instruction to the child. She soon drew a crowd, and Sam was pleased to see her enjoying herself with all the children. It was his first real opportunity to see her with kids, and she was definitely a natural. She was patient and funny and the kids seemed to adore her. *Not as much as I do,* Sam thought. Callie needed to have more children—a houseful.

He told her that when she finished up and rejoined

him. Callie smiled and blushed simultaneously. "I always imagined myself having lots of kids. I guess that's some sort of knee-jerk reaction to being an only child. You must be the exact opposite, what with six brothers."

"Not at all," Sam said as he placed his hand at the small of her back and guided her up the brightly painted stairs. "I loved coming from a large family. Now I've probably waited too long."

Callie scoffed. "You don't exactly look over the hill to me."

"I'm forty-one," Sam admitted.

"That's hardly old."

"Then why do I feel as if I'm a hundred?"

MRS. HARRINGTON wasn't what Callie had expected. With her athletic build, she didn't look a day over twenty-five.

"Sam," she said with a smile. "I haven't seen you in a while." Her smile faded. "I was sorry to hear about Mrs. Lange. How's Kevin holding up?"

Callie listened quietly as Sam provided a minimum amount of details.

"…Seth has agreed to place two deputies here, in plain clothing, anytime Kevin is here."

Mrs. Harrington smiled, but this time it was a sign of regret. "I'm sorry, Sam. I know he probably misses his friends, but look at it from my perspective. I have nineteen other children and five staff members to think of."

Sam surprised Callie by not arguing. *Was this the Sam she'd seen in action at his office?*

"I understand," he told Mrs. Harrington. "Since you can't allow Kevin to come back, perhaps you'd be willing to help me in another way."

"Anything," she said.

Callie suddenly realized that Sam had masterfully manipulated the woman. Smooth, very smooth.

"There was a man here about a month ago. I'm not sure what ruse he used, but he managed to get a copy of your enrollment."

Mrs. Harrington looked perplexed. "I'm sorry, Sam, but it wasn't a man."

"Excuse me?" Callie asked.

"It was a woman," Mrs. Harrington supplied.

"And what did she look like?" Sam asked.

"Medium height, slim but not skinny."

Callie gripped Sam's arm, recognizing the description. "Did she have dark hair?"

Mrs. Harrington nodded. "Perfectly styled, too. She said she was from the Department of Health and Human Services. She had identification."

"Did you notice anything about her? Maybe you saw her car or picked up on an accent?" Sam prompted.

"Sorry. The only thing that stands out in my mind is her makeup."

"Overdone, underdone, what?" Callie asked.

Sam leaned over and whispered, "Kidnapper-style is my guess."

Chapter Thirteen

"Heavy," Mrs. Harrington said. "Like maybe she had a skin condition. Is there a problem?"

"No," Sam assured her. "I'll keep in touch about Kevin."

"Wait," Mrs. Harrington said, then she opened her desk and pulled out a folded sheet of construction paper. "I was going to mail this. It's a card from all the kids and the staff for Kevin."

"He'll love it," Sam said, accepting the gift.

Callie's thoughts whirled between admiring Sam's way of getting the owner to explain how the enrollment list was pilfered, the implication that Jim York was connected to the kidnapper, and her growing knowledge of the wonderful world Sam had created for Kevin. She couldn't have asked for a better environment for her child than Little World. She wouldn't just be tearing Kevin away from Sam and all his uncles, she'd be ripping him from a world where he was loved and cherished.

She had to keep her thoughts to herself in front of

the day-care staff. "How much is this place a month?" she asked Sam as they descended the steps.

"It's $450.00 a week."

"I could never afford that," she mused.

Callie was treated to a chorus of cheerful goodbyes from the children. Several begged her to come back and paint with them. Julie stepped forward and said, "I've seen some of your paintings, Miss Walters. So I just wanted to tell you how great it was to have you share with the kids. Would you mind signing our celebrity board?"

"Celebrity?" Callie repeated, a little stunned.

Julie led her to the back of the main playroom. She felt a little like the Pied Piper since all the children followed behind them. She glanced at the bulletin board and noted the signatures of the governor, several *New York Times* bestselling authors, including her personal favorite, Nora Roberts. Dr. Chance Landry had signed as well as local television celebrity Chandler Landry. Callie was a tad overwhelmed as Julie handed her the marker. Racking her brain for several minutes, Callie finally decided on a quote from *The Unknown Wisdom of Jacqueline Kennedy Onassis:* "Children have been a wonderful gift to me and I am thankful to have once again seen our world through their eyes."

She signed her name, then hugged her way out of the building, where they found Chance leaning against Sam's Jaguar, sipping from a bottle of spring water.

"How goes it?" Chance asked.

Callie and Sam alternated bringing Chance up to speed. Chance's easy expression slipped for a moment as Sam provided him with the details on Mrs. Lange's funeral.

"I can't make it," Chance said. "I've got six kids with a resistant strain of strep I've got to keep tabs on, as well as a few appointments I just can't reschedule."

"I understand," Sam said, placing a hand on his brother's shoulder.

Chance turned his attention to Callie. "How are those stitches?"

"They itch," she admitted.

"When you get back from the funeral, maybe—"

"I'm not going," Callie interrupted. "I don't think I could face her family knowing it's my fault that she's dead."

Chance seem taken aback by her comment. "A lunatic killed her, Callie. Not you."

She shrugged. "I just wouldn't feel comfortable. I thought I'd use tomorrow afternoon as an opportunity to make some headway with Kevin."

"He's a great kid," Chance commented.

"To everyone but me."

She felt Sam drape his arm around her shoulders in a comforting gesture. "I keep telling her he'll come around."

"Then what?" Chance asked. After a deafening silence, he switched topics. "Tell you what, if things get rough at the ranch, come on in and I'll see if we can't take those stitches out a little early."

Callie's smile was genuine. ''That would be great.''

''Have you been taking your pills?''

''Yes,'' she answered.

''I've made sure she has,'' Sam added, making it sound as if he'd wrestled her to the ground and forced them down her throat.

Callie gave Sam a withering look, then turned to Chance and asked, ''Have you ever heard of a therapist named Molly Jameson?''

''Sure, she's top-notch.''

''Really?'' Callie asked.

''I happen to know her. Is there anything I can do to help?''

''Get us an appointment? Sam's new housekeeper—''

''The sexy-voiced Taylor Reese?'' Chance said on a laugh. ''She was all Shane talked about when I called out to the ranch this morning. She answered the phone. She does have a sexy voice.''

''You all are terrible,'' Callie chided. ''She wants a job so she can finish college. If last night was any indication, her focus is school, not picking her favorite Landry brother.''

Chance raised his hands. ''Shane already called dibs.''

Callie laughed. ''I can't believe you. You're a doctor, not some adolescent competing for the prom queen.''

Sam held her closer. ''She's right. You and Shane

should know better. But in case you don't, I have dibs on Callie.''

She shoved him, just as a giddy feeling filled her. ''I don't want to be *dibbed*.''

Sam leaned forward and whispered into her ear. ''You already were dibbed. If I may say, it was the best dibbing of my life.''

''Sam!'' she warned, though she was laughing. ''Can we continue on with our errands, please?''

''I'll give Molly a call,'' Chance promised. ''I'll see you tomorrow, Callie.''

''Thanks.'' She got in the passenger's side of the car.

While she waited for Sam to join her, she looked up at the day-care center and saw a half dozen little faces pressed against the windows. She waved, and the gesture was returned tenfold.

''I think they liked you,'' Sam said as he started the engine.

Still reeling from the idea that her P.I. might be connected to the kidnapper, Callie was grateful for the distraction. ''I liked them,'' she said. ''I've pretty much avoided children for the past three years, so I can't tell you how wonderful this morning was for me.'' When Sam didn't put the car in gear, she turned to him and asked, ''What?''

He was watching her with hooded, black eyes. His expression was still and serious as his gaze roamed over her features. Callie felt her heartbeat quicken and she suddenly felt warm. Very warm. It was amazing that all he had to do was look at her and her skin heated.

Reaching out, Sam traced the line of her jaw with his fingertip. Callie sat still.

"You have a beautiful mouth," he said as he reached across the armrest and rested his palm in the hollow of her cheek. His eyes fixed on her slightly parted lips, and Callie felt a rush of desire surge through her. His thumb began to gently caress her lower lip. Sam increased the pressure, his gaze never leaving her mouth. His touch became slightly rougher. It was intoxicatingly intimate. Maybe even more intimate than a kiss.

"Sam?" She wasn't sure whether she was going to tell him to stop or beg him to continue. She only knew that her breath had stilled in her throat. Her pulse, quick and uneven, raced through her veins carrying the thrill of his touch to every cell in her body.

"Thank you," Sam said as he pulled his hand away.

Callie wanted to reach out and pull his hand back to her face. Her internal battle continued well after Sam had pulled away from the curb. When she finally had control of her libido, she asked, "Why did you thank me?"

Sam kept his eyes on the road. His voice was quiet when he answered, "You let me touch you."

"That requires a thank-you?"

Taking one hand off the wheel, Sam reached out and let it rest on her thigh. She could feel the outline of his fingers as if she'd been branded. It was as if there was nothing in the universe except the thrill of having Sam's hand on her body. *I hope Chance gets me an appointment with the counselor soon. Obviously I need it!*

"I spent half of last night unable to sleep because of you."

"Sam?" Callie made his name a plea.

"Hear me out, please?"

"Okay."

"I think I've been pressing you too hard."

"You've been wonderful. I know it's hard, but you've been trying to build a bridge for Kevin and me."

"This isn't about Kevin," he insisted, clearly perturbed. "This is about *us.*"

"There can't be an us," Callie said, feeling incredibly sad as the words fell from her mouth. The same mouth that still tingled from the feel of his touch.

"What if you'd met me under other circumstances?"

"I *didn't* meet you under different circumstances."

She watched as his shoulders slumped dejectedly. "Will you at least give me a chance?"

Callie blew out a breath. "Kevin has to be my first priority right now."

"But does he have to be your only priority? You haven't allowed yourself to have a life since he was kidnapped."

"Forgive me if I didn't feel much like hitting the

bar scene when I didn't know where my baby was. If I heard on the news that a body had been found, I would go crazy until I knew it wasn't my son. I've spent virtually every moment of the past three years focused on finding my baby. It's not as though I can turn all that off in the course of a couple of days.''

"I'm not asking you to pretend the past three years weren't painful. I'm simply asking you to rejoin the world."

"Maybe you're asking too much," Callie responded. *Or maybe I'm just afraid.*

"Stop number two," Sam said when he parked in a lot marked for banking customers only.

"Why are we going to the bank?"

"I'm hoping someone will remember Lynn coming in and making those withdrawals."

"That was more than eight months ago," Callie cautioned.

"Maybe we'll get lucky," Sam said.

She followed him inside one of the oldest and most prestigious banks in all of Montana. The air was a battle of perfume, coffee and a cherry-scented commercial air freshener. Their footsteps echoed as they strode through the lobby of the historic building. Apparently it paid to be a Landry.

Sam was passed straight into the bank manager's office. A small, portly man with a very bad toupee stood and greeted them. He treated Callie as if she were local royalty. She wondered if now would be a good time to bring up the fact that his bank had refused to issue a credit card to her. Probably not.

"Frank, we have a problem," Sam said once they were seated in high-back leather chairs.

The bank manager paled. "Whatever it is, Sam, we'll get it straightened out immediately. We wouldn't want to fall out of favor with our favorite family."

Sam retrieved some papers out of the pocket of his suitcoat. "I'm interested in these withdrawals."

Frank produced a pair of half glasses and reviewed the documents. He then turned in his chair and began entering information into a computer. He swiveled the screen so Sam and Callie could view it. "All of the checks were made out to cash and endorsed by Mrs. Landry. Look here," he said as he split the screen so that the backs of the checks were on one side and a bank signature card was on the other. "The signature is genuine."

"I'm not disputing that my late wife cashed the checks. I'm hoping someone here might remember one of the occasions she came in to make a transaction."

Frank entered more information into the computer, then pressed the intercom button on his desk. "Send Marsha in here, please."

He smiled at Sam and Callie. "Apparently your wife liked one of our tellers. On almost all of the dates you've indicated, Marsha handled the transaction."

An elderly woman with frightened brown eyes slipped inside the room. She looked at everyone through the thick lenses of glasses enhanced by a faux pearl chain that hung around her neck. "You needed to see me, sir?"

"Do you remember Mrs. Landry?" Frank asked.

"Of course," she answered. "I'm sorry for your loss, Mr. Landry."

Sam shrugged off the comment.

Frank gestured the woman around his desk and pointed at the computer screen. "Do you recall anything about these transactions?"

"Just that Mrs. Landry and her friend were always at my window first thing in the morning. Usually on the fifth or so of every month."

"Her friend?" Sam asked.

"Yes, sir," Marsha answered. "I never got her name, but she was medium height, small-boned and—"

"Brown hair and heavy makeup?" Callie asked.

"Why, yes, ma'am," Marsha answered, obviously surprised.

"You don't perchance have any videotape?" Sam asked. The bank manager apologized as he explained that they used a continuous loop tape and unless there had been an incident, they reused the same tape.

A few minutes later, they were back out in the chill of the day. Callie rubbed her arms as she waited for Sam to unlock the car door.

"Do you want my jacket?" Sam asked.

"I'm fine," Callie insisted. "Where to next?"

She watched as Sam pulled a rumpled sheet of paper from his pocket. "To Fourteenth and Main."

"Where did you get this?" Callie asked.

"I rubbed the image from a pad by York's telephone."

"And you didn't tell me?" Callie demanded.

"I'm telling you now."

Callie glared at him. "What happened to 'no more secrets'?"

Chapter Fourteen

"It wasn't a secret," Sam insisted.

Callie lifted his hand off her leg and tossed it back in his direction. "What do you call not telling me what you found at Jim York's place?"

"I was in a hurry to get out of there. I planned on showing it to you and discussing it with you later, but then we had that scene with your father and... This is it," he said as he stopped briefly at the corner of Fourteenth and Main. The car behind him gave a honk, so Sam pulled into the first empty spot along the road.

"Does this mean anything to you?" he asked Callie when she joined him on the sidewalk.

"All Things Male?" she said, reading the sign above the shop. "I've never heard of it."

"Maybe they've heard of Jim York." Sam reached for her hand, but she moved away. They walked side by side until Sam opened the door to the shop and followed Callie inside.

It was a small space with ceiling-to-floor postal

boxes on three of the four walls. The fourth wall had
a counter. Behind that, he could see an area set up
for packaging large items. When he closed the door,
a buzzer sounded, summoning a man in his mid-
twenties.

"Hi," Callie greeted.

"Hi," the man returned the greeting, his eyes still
on Sam. "How are you, sir? I'm Carlton. How can
I help you?"

"I'm fine," Sam answered. "We're looking for a
friend."

"You came to the right place," Carlton replied
with a wink. The phone rang, and he excused himself
for a minute.

"He seems helpful."

Callie snickered. "You haven't caught on yet,
have you, Sam?"

"Caught on to what?"

"The name of the store? The counter guy checking
you out from fifty paces? Any of this ringing any
bells?"

"We're in a gay mailbox place?" Sam inquired
softly.

Callie grinned and nodded. "That's my guess."

"I'm back," Carlton said. "What can I do for
you?" He took out an order pad and pulled the pencil
from behind his ear.

"I think a friend of mine does business here. Jim
York?"

Carlton shook his head. "Name doesn't sound familiar. Describe him."

"Short," Sam said. "Balding, green eyes."

Carlton shook his head.

Callie stepped forward and said, "What about a woman? Medium height, slender—"

"Brown hair and drag-queen makeup?" Carlton finished. "She's been in once. Yesterday."

"Does she have a box?" Sam asked.

"She had a key," Carlton said. "She took a letter out of that box over there." He pointed to a small-size box on the third row from the top.

"Can you tell me who owns that box?" Sam asked.

Carlton was about to say no when Sam slipped a hundred-dollar bill across the counter.

"I really shouldn't," he hedged as he took the hundred. "I can tell you that no one has used that box for a while."

Sam slipped another hundred across the counter. "This is for details," Sam warned.

Carlton reached under the counter and produced a ledger book. "She's had the box for almost three years. The last rent was paid a year in advance this past January."

"By whom?" Sam asked, his patience running thin.

"A Mrs. S. Landry. She used to come in kinda regularly. Sometimes she had a kid with her. Sometimes not. She was always dressed and had great fingernails. I'll bet she had them manicured every other day."

"Was she a strawberry blonde?" Sam asked.
"About five-ten?"

"That's her. Now I don't feel so bad telling you," Carlton smiled with relief. "I guess you did know her."

"You could say that," Sam muttered as he took Callie's hand. "I was married to her."

"MOLLY WILL BE HERE in about a half hour," Taylor said when they arrived back at the ranch.

"We'll be in the study," Sam said, indicating that Callie should follow him.

"Daddy!" Kevin squealed with delight as he ran full steam into Sam's legs.

Sam responded in ritual fashion. He pretended to fall to the ground, then when Kevin went to check him, he got up, and tossed Kevin in the air. The boy giggled all through it.

"Were you good for Taylor?" he asked.

"Very, very, very, very good!" Kevin exclaimed as he wiggled out of Sam's hold. "I'm playing with my red guy. Hi, Callie!" he called before disappearing into the playroom.

He turned and saw Callie on the verge of tears. Smiling, he said, "I told you he'd come around."

"I want to hold him so badly."

"Here," Sam said. "I'll act as stand-in. I could use a hug after today."

This wasn't a sexual contact, Sam decided as he gently stroked her silky hair. Holding Callie gave him strength and made him feel…different. Lynn was secrets and deceits. Callie was honesty and warmth. How could he ever have confused what he felt for Lynn with the way Callie made him feel? *This has to be love.* "You smell good," he said against her hair.

"So do you," she replied in a near whisper. "But you always smell good."

She reached her hands inside his jacket and flattened her palms against his chest. His heartbeat instantly quickened. It echoed in his ears, and he was sure she could hear it, too. "I can't believe I'm going to say this, but we need to finish talking before the shrink gets here."

Callie withdrew slowly, her fingers lingered on him just a fraction too long for it to have been an accident. That was promising, Sam hoped.

"We have to figure out if Jim York is connected to the kidnapping," Sam said. "The woman who got the day-care list, the woman with Lynn at the bank and the woman at the mailbox place all match the description of the kidnapper. If Jim knows her, he could have known where to find Kevin the entire time Lynn and I were married."

"So why did he let me hire him?" Callie wondered aloud, clearly hurt.

"Maybe to keep you from hiring someone who might really find Kevin." It was obvious to Sam that Callie never expected the worst from anyone, and was always pained when anything bad happened. That explained why she was so ambivalent about the man who had abandoned her when she was pregnant.

It also explained how she managed to cope with her screwball father. Sam's admiration grew. In spite of all the pain and hurt, Callie still held on to the belief that people were inherently good. All people. So again he asked, "What about Mary? She recommended Jim."

Callie looked even more stricken. "She *never* would have let me suffer if she knew where my son was."

Sam didn't argue, but he wasn't sure he agreed. "So who the hell is this woman we keep hearing about?"

"Got me," Callie said on a breath. "I can't think of anyone who fits her description. I couldn't identify her from the hospital video, either."

"No one came to look at your paintings? Think hard."

"I am," she assured him. "What about you? Did an overly made-up woman come to you for financial counseling?"

They were interrupted when Taylor brought Molly Jameson into the office.

Sam thought Molly looked awfully young to be giving advice about life, but he had agreed to let Callie select the therapist, and Chance thought highly of her. "Take this seat," Sam suggested, relinquishing his chair behind the desk.

"I don't usually see people in their homes, but when Chance explained the general situation to me, I felt it was best if we got started immediately."

"Thank you, Dr. Jameson," Callie said.

"Please call me Molly," she insisted as she pulled a tablet from her briefcase. "Where is the little boy?"

"Kevin is playing," Sam answered. "Do you want me to get him?"

"Not yet," Molly said. "Let me spend some time with the two of you first. Sam, how about if I start with you. Callie, would you mind excusing us for a little while?"

As soon as Callie left, Sam was asked to retell the story of how he came to be Kevin's father. Molly went over everything. His marriage, his feelings about his absent parents, even his relationships with his brothers. It seemed as though she wanted to know about everything except why Kevin should stay with him.

"Send Callie in now, please."

Sam did as asked, though he had a strong urge to get a glass and listen at the door. Instead, he joined Taylor and Shane in the kitchen. He watched the seconds tick away on the clock. He felt as if it took two years for the forty minutes to pass and he was finally asked to return, this time with Kevin.

"Kevin, this is Molly. She's a doctor," Sam explained as he settled in the chair with Kevin on his lap.

"'Lo," Kevin said. "Like Uncle Chance?"

"I'm a different kind of doctor," Molly explained. "I'm a talking doctor. All we do is talk."

Kevin nodded.

Molly asked him some pretty benign questions, his

favorite foods, his favorite toys. She spent about ten minutes just chatting with Kevin, who was getting a little restless. Sam mouthed his concerns about Kevin's attention span to Molly.

"Tell me about your mommy, Kevin."

He shrugged. "She's in heaven."

"Before she went to heaven. Was she a good mommy?"

"Yeah."

"She didn't yell at you?"

Kevin shook his head. "She only yelled at Daddy and at the lunch lady."

"Who is the lunch lady?" Molly asked.

"She had some lunch with us sometimes after school."

"He means Little World," Sam corrected. "But who is she?" Sam pressed. "What's her name, honey?"

Kevin shrugged.

Molly looked up at Sam and said, "Mr. Landry, I'll ask the questions, okay?"

Sam grudgingly nodded.

"How did it make you feel when Mommy yelled?"

Kevin shrugged. "I liked it when she yelled at the lunch lady 'cause she was mean. She was very, very mean and didn't like me."

"How was the lunch lady mean?"

"She just was," Kevin said. "She wouldn't talk to me even when I was good. Not like Daddy. It made me mad when Mommy yelled at Daddy."

Kevin lifted his face to Sam and said, "I don't like to talk anymore."

"One more question, Kevin. Last one," Molly said. "How would you feel about living in a different house."

"I live in this house." Kevin announced before squirming down to the floor and racing out, but not before slamming the door.

"He's a very well-adjusted little boy," Molly said.

"So he'll be okay if I take him home?" Callie asked.

Sam felt his gut knot as he waited for the response.

Molly let out a slow breath, then said, "I'm sorry, Callie, but my professional opinion is no."

Sam felt like jumping for joy, but contained himself out of deference to Callie. "How do you suggest we proceed?" Sam asked.

"Slowly," Molly answered.

Callie was silent.

"I think it would be best if we approached this situation slowly and carefully. He's already suffered two major losses in his life. I think another one so close on the heels of losing Mrs.—" Molly stopped and read her notes "—Lange, could result in some long-term emotional problems."

"So I'm supposed to leave him here?" Callie asked, her voice shaky.

"For a while," Molly opined. "But Sam has indicated to me that you are welcome to stay here, as well. Which, in the long run, is the best possible situation."

"Really?" Callie scoffed.

Molly's brows drew together with apparent concern. "Is there a problem between the two of you? I don't think it's good for Kevin to be in a tense environment. You heard that one of his strongest memories of his…mother was arguing. If you two can't be civil, well—"

"We can," Sam insisted. "Callie just doesn't believe that I've fallen in love with her."

"Oh," Molly breathed. "Callie?"

"He's known me for a week. He can't possibly love me."

"What about you?"

Sam was cheated out of hearing that answer by the ringing telephone. He grabbed the receiver and fairly barked, "Hello!" into the line.

"This is your last warning," a raspy voice said.

"Who the hell are you?" Sam demanded, oblivious to the fact that his raised voice had caught the attention of both women.

"I killed Lynn, I can kill Callie or Kevin. Or both."

The line went dead.

Chapter Fifteen

Seth and two deputies and a technician were in the house in under a half hour. Dr. Jameson stayed only long enough to verify the time of the call.

"Did you get Caller ID?"

Sheepishly Sam said, "I forgot to arrange it."

His brother gave him an exasperated look. "Has anyone used the phone since the call came in?"

"No," Callie answered. "I made Sam use his cell phone because I think there is something you can dial to call back the number."

Sam felt a twinge of jealousy when Seth kissed Callie's cheek and said, "Brains and beauty. Way to go."

The technician pulled out a briefcase that housed a rather impressive bunch of equipment and some headphones. He partially disassembled the receiver to attach wires with alligator clips. The whole thing took less than ten minutes.

Sam watched as Seth dialed, then handed the

phone to him. "If he answers, keep him on the line as long as possible for the trace."

The phone was answered on the third ring.

"Hello?"

"Who is this?" Sam asked, knowing instantly that he wasn't speaking to the person with the indistinguishable voice and distinctive threats.

"Who is this?" the caller shot back. Sam handed the phone to Seth saying, "It isn't him. Maybe you can get some information from this person."

It seemed natural to Sam to go to Callie and put his arms around her. It seemed just as natural when, in turn, she slipped her arm around his waist. Anger was simmering in the pit of his stomach. He'd had about as much as he cared to take from the lunatic.

After identifying himself, Seth appeared to have more luck with the person who answered the phone. He asked several questions, then replaced the receiver and looked at the technician. "Route 151 near Deer Lodge?"

The technician nodded.

"You can pack it in." Seth turned to the deputies. "I want you by the entrance. Don't let anyone in here without checking with someone here at the house. You," he continued to the other deputy, "are to stay parked in the driveway. I want this house watched twenty-four hours a day."

"What about Kevin?" Callie asked. "Won't the police cars frighten him?"

"Naw," Seth said. "He's used to my car. He'll probably just bug you to go out and play with the lights and the siren.''

"I've got men posted already," Sam said.

"Keep 'em posted."

"Let me make you a thermos of coffee," Taylor offered the two deputies. She looked over at Sam and asked, "Is there something I can get for you all?"

"Just coffee," Seth answered.

Callie said, "Nothing."

Sam knew what he wanted wasn't in the kitchen. He left Seth and Callie in the living room, then went up to check on Kevin. He was fast asleep. Sam knew he had Taylor to thank for that. Taylor had fed him and put him to bed while Sam and Callie were with Dr. Jameson. Stroking Kevin's hair away from his tiny face, Sam whispered, "It looks like you aren't going anywhere for a while, pal. I love you." He kissed Kevin's forehead then went to leave the room.

"Love you, too," he heard Kevin reply in a groggy little voice. By the time Sam had turned to his son, Kevin was back asleep.

He made a stop by the bar in the office before joining Seth and Callie. On the way he noticed that Shane was still in the kitchen, probably annoying Taylor. Obviously his baby brother didn't know when to quit. *Like you do?* his brain challenged as he took a seat next to Callie on the sofa.

"The kid can't hear us, right?" Seth asked.

"He's zonked," Sam assured him.

"Tell me exactly what the guy said about Lynn," Seth began, referring to the phone call.

"I'm not sure it's a guy," Sam corrected, then took a sip of bourbon.

"Whatever."

"Anyway, he said he had killed Lynn and would kill Callie and Kevin if I didn't stop looking for him—or her."

"I thought your wife died in a car accident," Callie said.

"She did." Sam looked over and saw Seth's brow furrowed as if in deep thought. "Right?"

"She lost control of her van on a curve. But remember, there wasn't any brake fluid in the system."

"*You* told me the forensics people had gone over the brake line with a fine-tooth comb and didn't find any evidence of tampering. *You* told me it was an accident."

"Lighten up, Sam," Seth warned. "I'm on your side."

"Sorry," Sam muttered.

Callie placed her hand on his thigh. If it was meant to calm him, it wasn't exactly working. Her touch was distracting.

"Is it possible for someone to have drained the brake fluid without it being detected?" Callie asked Seth.

"Maybe," he answered. "Unfortunately, the van was towed to a scrap yard east of town. I wonder if it's still there."

"After more than eight months?" Sam scoffed. "It was probably crushed and sold shortly after the accident."

"I'll check on it. Maybe we'll get lucky."

"I don't understand this," Callie admitted.

Sam heard the strain in her voice. He reached down and laced his fingers with hers. "It is a little confusing."

"Maybe the two of you should stop playing amateur detectives," Seth suggested. "Whatever you're doing is pissing this guy off big-time. Who besides family knows what is going on?"

"We told a lot of it to Dr. Jameson," Callie answered. "We took Kevin by to see my stepmother. I'm sure neither one of them is involved."

Sam tried to couch his question diplomatically. "Is there any reason Mary would have told David that you'd found your son?"

Callie shrugged. "I guess it's possible, but I've already told you, David was never interested in Kevin."

"David?" Seth asked.

"Kevin's sperm donor," Callie answered. "He never wanted Kevin in the first place. Besides, there's no connection between David and Lynn. David wouldn't have the guts to kill anyone."

"Does he know anything about cars?" Seth asked.

"He's the president of Johnson Motors."

"That makes him a pencil pusher, not a mechanic."

Callie lifted her eyes to Sam, "Actually, David was a mechanic at Johnson Motors. That's how he met Brittany."

"I DON'T KNOW if I can do this," Callie said to him the next morning when they were in the car on their way to see David Leary.

Sam managed to offer her a quick smile. "Your call. I can speak to him alone."

"No," Callie said on a breath. "I'll know if David is lying, you won't."

"You're sure?" Sam asked when he pulled into the lot of Johnson Motors.

Callie nodded, but he could see reservation in her beautiful eyes.

Sam had to blow off three salesmen on the way to the president's office on the second floor. An attractive brunette sat at the receptionist's desk. She looked to be medium height, had brown hair and wore a lot of makeup. He felt Callie squeeze his hand.

"May I help you?"

"I'd like to see David," Callie answered.

"Do you have an appointment?"

"No, but David is my brother."

"I see," she said with a smile. "I'll tell him you're here. Reaching under her desk, the receptionist pulled silver crutches out, fitted them to her arms and went to the door marked Private.

"No one mentioned a handicap," Sam whispered after seeing the woman's severely mangled legs. "It's a little too obvious for anyone to have missed."

"...can forget it!" The office door slammed and Sam and Callie were looking into the face of Brittany Johnson. A very angry Brittany Johnson. There was just a flash of recognition before she bolted down the stairs.

"Callie?"

Sam turned and found himself staring at a man he had a strong urge to punch just on general principle. David Leary looked as though he had been born into the country club life-style. His blond hair was perfectly moussed into place. He was tanned, even though it hadn't been above fifty degrees out for weeks. His nervous smile revealed perfectly capped teeth. His suit was Armani, as were his shoes. Brittany had done a nice job of turning a mechanic into a president.

"Come in," David said with the fake pleasantness of a salesman. "How long has it been, Callie?"

Sam shut the door behind them.

"Not long enough," Callie replied sweetly.

David's facade of perfection threatened to slip. "I know things between us didn't end well, but my mother tells me you're earning a living painting. Isn't that what you've always wanted?"

"For the past three years, all I've wanted was my son."

At least Leary had the decency to erase the smile from his face. "That was a tough break" was his lame response. "And you are?"

"Sam Landry."

David's eyes perked up. "I see you've done pretty well by yourself, Callie. Nice to meet you, Mr. Landry. I think you know my wife."

"I know Brittany," Sam answered curtly. "Did

you know I've been raising the child you abandoned for the past three years?''

"How did that happen?" David asked. "I thought Mother said the child had been kidnapped by a woman." He turned his attention to Callie. "The police were all over me for a week. It really upset Brittany."

"God forbid," Callie muttered under her breath.

"So how did you end up with…"

"Him," Callie supplied.

Hearing the anger in her voice only renewed Sam's desire to kick the guy's butt.

"By the way," David said, "what happened to your face? You look awful."

"I was beaten," she replied. "You wouldn't happen to know anything about that, would you?"

David seemed genuinely shocked by her question. "Me? Why would I want you beaten?"

Sam reached into his suit coat and retrieved a piece of paper. "I want this signed and witnessed now."

"What is it?" David asked as he grabbed the papers out of Sam's hand.

Callie gave him a questioning look, but he silently asked for her patience. David buzzed in his receptionist, had her witness the document, then handed it back to Sam.

"Is there anything else?" David asked, all pretext of courtesy gone.

"Yes. Did you or Brittany know my wife? Lynn?" Sam asked.

"I didn't and I'm sure Brittany didn't."

"How can you be sure?" Callie asked.

"Brittany and I know all the same people," David said. "We don't have secrets."

"So you told her that you got Callie pregnant and left her to fend for herself?" Sam asked.

David glared at him. "Brittany was aware of the situation."

"Since when?" Callie asked.

"She found out when I did, thanks to you leaving me that detailed message on my machine."

"Gee, sorry," Callie said, without sounding the least bit apologetic.

"Where did Brittany run off to?" Sam asked.

David's glare turned into blatant hostility. "I will not permit you to upset my wife. That whole baby thing was very difficult for her."

"I can imagine," Callie breathed.

"I've signed your paper, I don't know your wife, and I'm happy you found your kid. Is there anything else?"

"I'll let you know," Sam promised.

As soon as they went down to the showroom, Callie demanded to see whatever it was Sam had asked David to sign.

"He just relinquished all his parental rights," Sam explained. "I had the attorney at my office draw up the papers and fax them to me early this morning."

Callie gaped up at him.

Sam took her hand and pulled her into an alcove

in the hallway between the showroom and the service area. "What's wrong?"

"Do you know what you just did?"

"I made sure that Leary isn't a part of Kevin's life. I thought that's what you would want."

"Emotionally, it is. But financially is another matter. You just let him out of paying child support."

Sam rolled his eyes. "I'll support you and Kevin."

"Is this a new tack you're using to try to keep Kevin?"

Sam raked his fingers through his hair. "No. I'm Kevin's father. I don't care about DNA. If anyone is going to support him, it will be me."

"But he isn't yours," Callie said softly.

"You're wrong, Callie, he is mine. He's ours."

Callie pressed her fingertips to her temple. "You're confusing me, Sam. Dr. Jameson already said I shouldn't take Kevin for a while. I agreed to abide by her advice. You didn't need to have David sever his parental rights."

"Yes I did."

"Why?"

"I don't want another man to lay claim to *my* son."

"In the future would you mind running this sort of thing past me first?"

"Promise," Sam said, making a cross sign over his heart. "Let's go visit the mechanics."

"Why?"

"I want to know if Lynn had her van serviced here."

"David said—"

"I don't care what he *said*. Do you trust him?"

Callie shook her head. "After Jim York, how can I trust anyone?"

Sam went to the service desk and asked to see the manager. A portly man with white hair greeted him. "You belong to that Jaguar out front?"

"Guilty," Sam said. "But I'm interested in finding out if my wife brought her van in here for service."

The man gave Callie a puzzled look. "I...um... can't remember when I last had the car serviced."

He shook his head and winked at Sam. "I know how frustrating it is when the wife gets forgetful. I've been in the car business for near on forty years and she still doesn't remember to get the oil changed every three months."

"You know how we silly women can be," Callie said, saccharin dripping off each word.

Sam squeezed her hand in warning. "As you can see, my wife had a nasty accident recently."

"Musta been a doozy," he replied.

"It's left her a little fuzzy."

"Fuzzy?" Callie repeated.

"Yes, dear. Don't you remember just last week when I had to show you where the bed was?"

Callie blushed and lowered her head. Sam didn't want to embarrass her, he just wanted to shut her up while he still had the cooperation of the service manager.

He went into a back room and came out with the service book for the month of Lynn's accident. After nearly twenty minutes of searching, he found no record of Lynn's van by license plate, number or name.

"Thanks for checking," Sam said.

"No problem. I saw you go up to the boss's office. I figured he'd want me to do whatever you asked. Sorry I wasn't more help."

"Actually," Sam began, "you could help me with a problem I've been having with my new van." He described the make and model.

"Sure thing."

"The brake fluid keeps leaking out, but I can't find the leak."

"Bring it in. My guess is the coupler is probably loose. If you can't find any leaks in the hose, then the fluid is probably leaking from the connection to the fluid container."

"Does it come out all at once?" Sam asked. "I haven't noticed any spots on the driveway.

"Little by little," he said.

"Thank you," Sam said, then turned to leave.

"Sure. You know, you're the second person who's asked me about brake lines on that kind of van. The first time was about a year ago."

Sam stopped cold. "Really? Maybe it's a factory defect or something. Do you remember who asked you?"

Chapter Sixteen

"I don't believe this," Sam grumbled when they were back in the car and headed for the ranch.

Callie touched the sleeve of his suit and said, "I know. We keep getting the same description. Brown hair, medium height, slender, too much makeup."

"If only the service manager had remembered the woman's name."

"But he didn't," Callie mused. "It's amazing he even remembered what she looked like after all this time. If I hear her described one more time I'm going to spit."

Sam brought her hand to his mouth and kissed her palm. "For a minute there, I thought we were finally going to know her name." Sam shook his head. "This woman has been seen at the hospital, taking Kevin. At his day care, at the mailbox place. Someone has to know her."

"I'll ask Chance if he's seen her," Callie suggested. "Wouldn't it be wonderful if she was one of his patients?"

"It would be wonderful if she was dead."

Callie felt as if she had all the pieces of the puzzle, but didn't have them in the right order. All the way back to the ranch, she and Sam brainstormed about the mysterious woman. Unfortunately, by the time they reached the Lucky 7, they were no closer to guessing her identity than they had been earlier.

"I just put Kevin down for a nap," Taylor said when she greeted them at the door.

Callie was disappointed. She wanted to start spending more time with her son. Maybe after his nap.

Sam ate the sandwich Taylor made for him. Callie just picked at the lettuce.

"Why aren't you eating?"

"I'm thinking," she answered.

Sam gave her that sexy half smile, then asked, "Can't do two things at once?"

She grinned back at him. *Do I love him? Is that possible after such a short time? I've mistakenly put my faith in three people so far. How do I know this is right?* "Normally I can juggle several balls in the air at once. Right now I feel as though I have the solution on the tip of my tongue, but I can't get it out.

Sam came over to her and cupped her face. He kissed her. It was a mind-shattering experience.

He lifted his head long enough to say, "There is nothing on the tip of your tongue," before he deepened the kiss.

Before she realized it, Sam was carrying her up

the steps to his bedroom. He stopped long enough to shut the door with his foot before he placed her on the bed.

"I love you," Sam whispered, then he made love to her.

Amazingly, it was even better than the first time. This time she didn't feel the weight of guilt. She only felt…cherished.

"You're smiling," Sam said as he lifted himself up on one elbow and touched his fingertips to her lips.

"So are you," she countered, then she kissed his fingers, each in turn.

"Tell me you love me," Sam said, holding her gaze.

Callie closed her eyes. "I can't do that yet, Sam. I can't say it until I'm sure."

There was a slight sadness in his eyes, but his smile remained. "I'll take that for now."

"Good." She started to snuggle up to him, thinking a nap would be a wonderful idea.

"I have to go," Sam said regretfully. "I've got the funeral this afternoon."

Callie almost cringed. "I forgot, I'm sorry. How awful of me to be enjoying myself when Mrs. Lange's family is preparing to bury her."

"Stop beating yourself up with guilt," Sam insisted. "I feel some of it, too, but Seth is right. We didn't kill her, some lunatic did."

Callie lay in the bed and enjoyed watching Sam dress. Technically, she enjoyed seeing him naked, but there was something intimate about watching him select a tie. *It would be easy to get used to this,* she thought. *Maybe too easy.*

"You're frowning," Sam observed. "Please don't go feeling guilty on me."

"I'm not," she assured him. "I'm just afraid that all this is too easy."

"Easy?"

She nodded. "I feel as if I've traded my unhappy life for a fairy-tale one."

"Good." He kissed her forehead. "I want you to feel like a princess. I want to love you and cherish you while we grow old together."

"That's the problem," Callie admitted. "You have everything in the world to offer me, and I don't have anything to offer you."

"That's ridiculous," Sam countered dismissively. "You make me feel alive, Callie. I was so gun-shy after Lynn that I'd forgotten how wonderful it could be to fall in love. And you have something very special to offer me."

"Like?"

"A brother or sister for Kevin. But I insist you marry me first."

"Whoa." Callie held up one hand. "I can't even think in terms of altars and babies yet. Be patient with me, Sam. Let me sort my feelings out."

"I'll try to be patient," he said. "At least for a few days."

Callie tossed a pillow at him as he ducked out the door. Slowly she dressed and went to her room, where she bathed and changed before going down-stairs.

Kevin was in his playroom. Callie stood in the doorway watching him for a few moments. He was so perfect, so beautiful. It was hard to believe that her body had produced such an incredible child. Sam wanted more children, she remembered.

So do I.

Sam said he loved her.

I think I love him, too.

She and Sam and Kevin could be a family.

I want a family.

Sam wanted to get married.

The therapist said it was best for Kevin to be with them both.

"Want to play?" Kevin asked.

Callie's heart sang. "Sure. What are we playing?"

"What do you like to play?"

"I like to draw," Callie said.

"Me, too. I have a pad and some crayons."

"How about if I draw a picture of you?"

Kevin shrugged. "Sure. I'm going to draw kittens."

Callie took a sheet from the pad, and her eyes volleyed between Kevin and the image she was creating on the page. "I'm finished," she said after adding a hint of yellow for his hair.

"Wow!" Kevin exclaimed. "You're a good drawer person."

"Thanks. Let me see yours."

Kevin frowned. "It isn't good."

"Let me see." Kevin handed over his drawing. It wasn't bad for a three-year-old. "You did a good job," she praised.

"Doesn't look like the kittens."

"If you get another piece of paper and come sit on my lap, I can help you draw the kittens."

Kevin eyed her cautiously. He got the paper, but kept his distance. "Draw them, please."

It took Callie about ten minutes to do a rough sketch of the kittens they had seen at Mary's the previous day. Kevin was delighted. Much to her chagrin, he couldn't wait to run and show the kittens to Taylor.

"I made headway," she said as she cleaned up the crayons and paper. She brought the drawing of Kevin into the kitchen and used a magnet to hang it on the refrigerator.

"You are *good*," Taylor commented.

"Put the kitties up, too!" Kevin demanded. "Then Daddy will remember to get me some when they can live with me."

Callie called Chance's office and was told to come in around four-thirty to get out the stitches. It was in the heart of town, so she figured she'd be safe. She had a little less than an hour before she had to leave, so she decided to stay and chat with Taylor in the kitchen. Kevin had raced off to watch a program on public TV.

"You're winning him over," Taylor said.

"Not fast enough. I wish he'd taken to me the way he has to you."

"What can I say," Taylor quipped. "Children and animals love me."

"What about men?"

"I've sworn off men. What about you?"

Callie chewed her lip for a minute before answering. "I don't know."

"Sure you do," Taylor countered. "Maybe you aren't ready to acknowledge your feelings yet, but you know."

"I don't think I like living with a psych major."

Taylor laughed. "It doesn't take a genius to see the vibes between you and Sam."

"We don't have vibes."

"Oh." Taylor sighed. "Then I guess you two were upstairs having casual sex?"

Callie felt herself blush all the way to the roots of her hair. That made Taylor laugh again.

"Don't be embarrassed," she counseled. "If a man treated me the way Sam treats you, I'd be walking on the wild side myself."

"He is an incredible man."

"So, are you headed for happily ever after, or what?"

"I don't know yet," Callie admitted. "I'm afraid I'm confusing my feelings about Kevin with my feelings about Sam."

"Excuse me?"

Callie blew out a breath. "Am I drawn to Sam because Kevin loves him, or is it the real thing?"

"Looks pretty real to me. I've got to get some ironing done."

"Sorry," Callie muttered. "I didn't mean to keep you from your work."

"You didn't. I enjoyed the conversation. It's a lot better than Shane's lame come-ons."

Callie went into the den where Kevin was watching television. He didn't seem to object when she sat beside him. While Kevin watched television, Callie watched him. Occasionally she would glance around the room. She spotted the wedding picture and decided to torture herself and go get a closer look.

Sam's first wife had a regal look about her. She was tall, slender and incredibly beautiful. In the shelves, Callie discovered a collection of photo albums. She couldn't resist. Afraid she might cry in front of Kevin, Callie carried them into the office and began studying every page. It was like watching her son grow up in fast-forward. He appeared to be a happy child. All the hallmarks were covered. His first birthday, his first Halloween costume, his first Christmas.

The only thing missing appeared to be the first three months of his life. The three months before Lynn married Sam. "Where were you and how did you get my baby?" she wondered aloud.

"Callie?" Taylor stuck her head in. "This came for Sam—" she held up a rectangular package "—and I'm leaving now."

"Leaving?" Callie repeated, panicked.

"I have class tonight. Don't worry, one of those cute cowboys they have around here is taking me."

No problem, Callie thought. *I'll take Kevin with*

me. We're just going to the doctor. Surely Kevin wouldn't freak the way he had when they were alone in the cabin. At least she hoped not.

She said goodbye to Taylor. Doubt lingered, so she called down to the bunkhouse to see if one of the hands could drive her and Kevin into town. No one answered. Well she could cancel her appointment. ''Or maybe Kevin would like to go visit his uncle Chance.'' They'd be safe. She wasn't going in to ask about the mysterious kidnapper, after all.

When she broached the subject with him, Kevin seemed reluctant. It wasn't until she let him call Chance to verify that she was going to his office and not back to the cabin that he agreed.

Callie took the keys to the four-by-four off the hook in the kitchen. She found the tape player in Kevin's room and grabbed it along with some tapes.

The deputy stopped her at the gate. ''I thought you were supposed to stay put.''

Callie smiled at his concern. ''I've got a doctor's appointment,'' she explained, touching her hand to the bandage. ''I'll go there and come straight home. I've promised Kevin a grilled-cheese sandwich and ice cream for dinner.''

The deputy's eyes still held lingering concern. ''Sam was with me when I made the appointment. It's okay.''

''Don't stop for anyone,'' the deputy warned. ''Keep your doors locked and stay where there are people.''

''I will.''

Callie felt a little creepy driving alone along the highway. About halfway between the ranch and town, she remembered that Mrs. Lange had been shot while driving. Maybe this wasn't such a swift idea. She considered turning around and was startled when the car behind her honked its horn. She looked at the speedometer and realized that she was driving twenty miles under the speed limit. She quickly sped up but kept checking the car in the rearview mirror.

A chill ran down her spine. The car following closely behind had those tinted windows, making it impossible for Callie to make out the driver.

She was still ten miles from Jasper.

She checked the console and the glove box but found no phone. The only thing she could do was speed up. The sooner she got to Jasper, the better. Callie kept her foot on the gas as the car reached a speed of eighty. Still the following car kept pace.

She was five miles from Jasper.

Callie tried to slow down enough so that she could get the license plate. It did no good. No matter her speed, the car kept the same distance. She thought about Sam. He'd be devastated if anything happened to Kevin. And poor Kevin. She almost cried at the mere thought of harm coming to her beautiful son.

She reached Jasper and took the turn onto Main Street on two wheels. The sedan with the tinted windows continued straight on the highway. Callie took her first relaxed breath in ten miles.

"That was fun!" Kevin cried. "Do it again!"

"I'm glad you enjoyed it," Callie said. "But it

really isn't safe to drive that fast around a corner. I did the wrong thing.''

''Will Daddy punish you?''

Probably, she thought. ''I don't think so.''

''There he is! There he is!'' Kevin sang loudly as he began waving to Chance, who was lingering in the doorway to his office.

Callie parked in the lot adjacent to the building. She lifted Kevin out of his car seat and started to carry him. Kevin had a different idea.

''Put me down!'' he yelled. Squirming in her arms until she had no choice but to comply.

''Hold my hand, there's traffic.''

Kevin ignored her completely and ran to the edge of the building. Callie raced after him, catching up just as Chance reached him.

''He's quick,'' Callie said through labored breaths.

''He sure is,'' Chance agreed before tossing Kevin into the air a few times. ''Come on in.''

Callie followed him into a cheery waiting room. The chairs were covered in bright, primary colors, and the walls were adorned with a mixture of factory recall notices, child's drawings and public health announcements.

She was introduced to Valerie, Chance's nurse, who quickly took Kevin into the X-ray room to look at the pictures of hands and feet.

''That's a pretty gruesome hobby,'' Callie commented.

''They're X-rays not autopsy photos,'' Chance said as he indicated she should enter one of his examination rooms. "Jump up on the table." Callie did as instructed. When Chance came over to her, his expression seemed to lose its cheerfulness. "Why are you sweating? And your hands are trembling."

Callie shrugged, embarrassed. "There was a car behind me almost all the way from the ranch. I guess I got spooked."

"I know the stitches itch, but I probably should have offered to come out to the ranch. I wasn't thinking."

"I don't need a house call," she insisted.

"I'll follow you back, all the same."

"That isn't necessary," Callie argued.

"Lie down so I can check the stitches." After she complied, he asked, "How are your ribs?"

"Fine."

"No problems with your vision?"

"No."

"I think we can take these out. I'll get some gloves and a suture remover and we'll be in business."

"Sounds wonderful."

Chance was very gentle, but it still stung a little. She was very happy when the ordeal was over.

"How much do I owe you?" Callie reached for her purse.

"On the house," Chance insisted. "Sam already paid the hospital bill."

Callie shook her head. "I'm not impoverished."

"Neither is he," Chance quipped. "He makes more than I do and *I'm* the doctor."

Callie reached into her purse and pulled out her nearly empty birth control pills and asked Chance for a refill.

Chance's mouth pulled into a tight line. "Didn't they ask you about medications when you were admitted to the hospital?"

A little taken aback by his stern abruptness, Callie answered, "Yes. I told them I didn't take anything."

Chance waved the birth control pills. "What are these, then?"

"I wasn't thinking about them. I only take them to keep my skin clear."

"Well," Chance sighed. "I hope you haven't had sex."

"Why?"

"Because the antibiotic I have you on negates the effectiveness of this brand of pills."

"But not immediately, right?"

"Wrong," Chance said.

Callie rubbed her face. "I don't believe this."

"I'll take that to mean you have had sex."

She blushed and nodded.

"Well, I guess you'll know soon. You're supposed to start your period tomorrow."

"Please don't say anything to Sam," she pleaded.

"I'll keep your confidence, Callie. Do I say I'm sorry or congratulations?"

"Don't ask me that just yet."

"If you need to talk, I'm a good listener," Chance offered. "But if you want my vote, you have it. I haven't ever seen my brother happier. You're obviously the right woman for him. I was wrong when I said you weren't his type. You are.''

''Thanks.'' Callie stammered anxiously, ''A-actually, I would like to ask you something.''

''Shoot.''

''Do you have a patient, female, medium height, brown hair, wears a lot of makeup?''

Sam shook his head. ''Nope. I'd remember a heavily made-up woman. From my single foray into makeup, I'm amazed by women who cake their entire face with that junk.''

Callie's mind reeled. ''Why did you wear makeup?''

''I was in a play at college. I'm not a closet crossdresser.''

''I don't know why I didn't think of it. I know who the woman is!'' Callie gushed. ''I'll go get the car, would you bring Kevin out?''

''Callie, what's the hurry?''

''I have to go see Seth. I'll explain later.''

She ran out to the car, opened the door, then felt the blow to the back of her head. The ground rushed up to her before everything went dark.

Chapter Seventeen

"Why didn't you watch her!" Sam demanded.

Chance offered nothing in response. His expression was apologetic, but Sam didn't want an apology, he wanted Callie.

Seth came in and said the state police had agreed to put up roadblocks. "Tell me exactly what happened."

"One minute we were talking about makeup and the next thing I knew she was flying out the door saying she needed to find you."

"Seth, not me?" Sam asked.

"No. She wanted to contact Seth."

"She told you about the woman?" Sam asked.

"The one with too much makeup, yeah. That's what we were talking about just before she left."

Sam felt frantic and helpless, and he didn't like either one of those feelings. An entire litany of horrible possibilities went through his mind. "Why did I leave her alone?"

"It isn't your fault," Chance insisted. "If anyone is responsible, it's me."

"No, it isn't either of you," Seth insisted. "And sitting around here passing out blame isn't doing any good. Chance, did you say anything to her that might have upset her?"

Chance didn't answer, Sam did. "He found the four-by-four in the parking lot with the door opened and some blood on the ground. Does that sound to you like she took off on her own volition?"

"I just wonder if she was distracted. If she was, that might explain why her guard was down."

"She wasn't distracted...*really*...until I told her I didn't have a patient who fit her description."

"What do you mean, *really?*" Sam demanded.

"A medical thing, Sam. I can't tell you what we discussed."

"Is she sick?" Sam had his brother by the lapels of his coat. "What's wrong with her?"

"Nothing," Chance insisted. "I can't tell you what we discussed, but I can tell you she doesn't have any illnesses."

"Thanks for the help," Sam grumbled. He followed the remark with a perfect punch. Chance crumpled to the living room floor.

Chance tested his jaw by moving it from side to side. Looking at Sam he said, "You get that one free, but don't take your frustrations out on my face."

"Sorry." Sam helped his brother to his feet.

"Getting into a brawl won't help," Seth said.

"Chance, something you said clicked with Callie. Can you remember the entire conversation?"

Chance repeated the story again, only this time he added, "I told her I'd worn makeup in a play in college."

"Christ!" Sam smacked his forehead. "It's not a woman!"

"Who?"

"It's got to be York!"

"The P.I.?" Seth asked.

"He's a small man but he'd be a medium-size woman. All it would take would be some makeup and a wig. He's very small-boned. Callie found traces of makeup in his trailer, and the first time I met him, he had a beige stain on his T-shirt."

"Are you sure?" Seth asked.

"I could be, if the FBI would send me the hospital videotape. I'm sure I would recognize him even in drag."

"I'll make a call."

Shane put his hand on Sam's shoulder. "Don't worry, we'll find her."

"I hope so," Sam sighed. "I asked her to marry me."

"That's good," Chance said.

"Not good. She didn't say yes."

"She turned you down?" Shane asked.

"Not exactly. I got a kind of 'check with me later' response."

Seth returned a minute later with news. "According to Agent Sinclair, the tape was delivered this afternoon.''

With Taylor out at class, Sam, Seth, Chance and Shane split up to search the house. Seth found the neatly wrapped tape on the office desk and yelled for the rest of the group.

Sam couldn't get down the stairs fast enough. It was the only time he could remember being upstairs at night and *not* checking on Kevin. But his son was safe. Callie wasn't.

IT WAS DARK. Very dark. Callie was hog-tied, but she could feel the rough surface beneath her cheek. It was bare floor. She heard nothing except the hum of the wind and the occasional sound of an animal. *Where am I?*

As if on cue, she heard the squeak of hinges as the door was opened. Cold air slapped her face.

''Who's there?'' she demanded.

Her answer was to be kicked on the side of her head. Bright stars danced before her blindfolded eyes.

''I've brought you some food and water,'' a raspy voice said. ''I'll untie you, but if you turn and try to look at me, I'll shoot you right now.''

Callie wasn't in any hurry to be shot, so when she was roughly rolled onto her side, she continued to face the wall long after her captor had left the room.

The minute she rolled over she recognized her prison. It was the hunting cabin on her father's ranch. Callie felt ill. Her own father had been behind everything? He had engineered the kidnapping? Written her all those taunting letters? Threatened everyone and killed Mrs. Lange? Callie was so overwhelmed that she began to sob. And where was Kevin? Safe with Chance, she hoped. She cried for what seemed like hours in the darkness.

Until she decided that crying wasn't going to set her free. She checked the window. It was nailed shut. The door was latched from the outside. She could pull it open just enough to see the outline of the lock. She knew her father kept it locked when he wasn't using it, mainly to keep trespassers from camping out in it or kids from trashing the place. What she wouldn't give for a teenager bent on mischief or a transient at that moment. The cabin was in the woods at the far edge of the property. There was no one around for miles, so screaming wasn't an option. She had to pick the lock or break the window. Then she would have to walk miles for help.

She decided to eat to build up her strength. At first light she'd make her escape. She lay down on the bare floor and thought of Sam and Kevin. Tears slid down her cheeks. She couldn't die now.

"THAT'S GOT TO BE YORK," Sam said after watching the videotape for the tenth time. "The build is the same. It's York."

"I'll call the FBI and get an APB out on him. What's the address of the trailer?"

Sam provided it and went into the kitchen to make another pot of coffee. It was then that he realized an early winter storm was blowing in. "If she's outside, she'll freeze to death," he told Chance.

"She isn't outside, Sam. Wherever York has her, I'm sure it isn't out in plain sight. Where did she find this York person, anyway?"

"Mary," Sam said. "I'll call her."

"It's three in the morning, Sam."

"I don't care." He reached for the phone, got the number from information, then dialed.

"What!"

"Mr. Walters, this is Sam Landry."

"Who?"

"Sam Landry. I was with Callie the other day when—"

"Don't call my house again!"

"She's missing."

There was nothing but silence on the other end.

"She was abducted from the parking lot next to my brother's office. We found blood."

"What am I supposed to do?" Walters asked, his tone a little less belligerent.

"I need to talk to your wife. I need to ask her about Jim York."

"Jim's a friend of ours."

"Do you know where he is?"

"No."

"The police think Jim York is involved in the kidnapping."

"That's nuts," Walters returned. "Why would Jim want to take a baby?"

"Maybe for you?" Sam suggested. It earned him

a dial tone. "Great! I guess I'll have to drive out there."

"Stay here until first light," Chance said. "This is a nasty storm, and you'll be no help to Callie if you end up in a ditch somewhere."

Sam knew his brother was right, he just couldn't stand the thought of doing nothing. The three hours until daybreak were the longest of his life.

"I'm going to see Mary," Sam announced.

"Me, too!" Kevin called as he raced into the kitchen. "I want to see the kitties again!"

"Not this time, pal. You have to stay here with Uncle Chance."

"But I want to see the kitties!" Kevin brooded.

"Another time," Sam insisted. "I have to go find your mother."

"My mommy's in heaven," Kevin said.

"No." Sam pulled Kevin on his lap. "She wasn't your real mommy, pal. She was being your mommy until Callie could find you. Callie is your mommy. Do you understand that?"

"Callie losted me?"

"Not exactly, honey. I'll explain everything to you after I find Callie, okay?"

"Where do you get a baby?" Kevin asked.

Chance reached for him and indicated Sam should go ahead. "I'll handle the baby question."

"Thanks," Sam said with genuine affection. "I've got my cell phone. Call me if anything happens."

"Hold on," Seth said. "I'm coming with you."

"Fine, if you're coming, come on. I'm not waiting."

Sam found himself a passenger in his brother's cruiser. The Jaguar wasn't great in heavy snow. And it was heavy. They'd gotten at least three feet during the night. *Where are you?* he pleaded in silence. *Please don't be dead.*

CALLIE WOKE TO FIND the window more than half-blocked by drifting snow. The wind whistled as it delivered frigid air to the cabin. Her feet were almost numb and her hands weren't much better. Her skirt and sweater were no match for a wicked Montana snowstorm. Her spirits plummeted. *Now what?*

All the firewood was outside, so there was no way to generate heat. Somehow she doubted that her father had given instructions that she be provided wood and blankets in the event of a storm.

She moved around, knowing that if she didn't keep moving, her body would give in to the hypothermia threatening. *I survive my son's kidnapping. I survive a beating. I survive an abduction and now I'm going to freeze to death. There's something pathetically ironic about that.*

"You aren't going to die," she said aloud. "You're going to find a way out of this. Just think!"

Callie checked all the drawers and cupboards and found nothing but a tin mug, an old pair of sunglasses and a map with her father's favorite hunting sites circled. Tearing the map, she wrapped the paper around her hands and feet. Then she paced, trying to think of a plan. She had to get back to Sam and Kevin.

SETH AND SAM ARRIVED at the Walters place a little before eight. Callie had been missing for fifteen hours. Sam struggled to clear a path in the snow to the door of the house. Mason Walters greeted him with the business end of a shotgun.

"Put the gun down," Seth ordered.

"You two are trespassing."

Seth came up and said, "You want to go to jail, sir?"

Walters grumbled, but finally let them in. Mary was seated at the table, her eyes red from crying. "Any word?" she asked.

"None," Sam said. "We need to know everything you know about Jim York."

"Do you think Jim took her?" Mary asked.

Sam nodded. "Apparently York was blackmailing my wife and either she refused to pay, or was afraid I'd get suspicious if she kept making withdrawals. For whatever reason, York fixed the brakes on her van and killed her. He's the prime suspect in the murder of my housekeeper, and he's the only one with a reason to want Callie dead."

"But why?" Mary repeated. "She has the baby back. Why would he want to kill her now?"

"Who knows. Maybe he realizes Callie won't quit until the man who took her baby is behind bars."

"I just can't see Jim doing these things you say," Walters said. "Mary's known him since school, and he's even done some work for my daughter-in-law. She's a Johnson, you know.''

''I know,'' Sam said. ''What kind of work did he do for her?''

Walters shrugged. ''I don't know. I just seen 'em with their heads together a time or two.''

Sam and Seth exchanged looks, then Seth went into the living room to arrange to have David and Brittany brought to the Walters'.

''Sam!'' Seth called. ''Come in here!''

Sam did as he was asked. ''What?''

Seth was holding the picture of Brittany taken at her college homecoming. ''Where did you say Lynn was from?''

''Ohio,'' Sam answered. ''Why?''

''See this?'' Seth said, pointing to the barely visible image of a hawk on Brittany's red shirt.

''So?''

''I watch a lot of college football. This is a Miami Redhawks shirt.''

''So? Callie told me she thought Brittany went to Miami.''

''This is Miami, but it's Miami, Ohio, not Florida.''

Sam went back into the dining room and said, ''Okay, game over.''

Walters blustered a bit, but when Sam ordered him to sit down and shut up, he complied.

''My dead wife was from Ohio. Your daughter-in-law went to college in Ohio. Your daughter-in-law wasn't thrilled with the idea of her fiancé having a child with another woman. My wife was unable to have children. Do you see a pattern here?'' Sam asked hotly. ''Lynn was paying York, you've seen Brittany with York? Jump in anytime.''

Sam was glaring at Walters, but it was Mary who broke into tears. ''It wasn't supposed to be like this.''

Chapter Eighteen

"What are you talking about?" Mason asked his wife. "You didn't have anything to do with this, did you?"

Mary was weeping softly. "No one was supposed to die." She repeated this over and over until Sam was ready to strangle her.

"Tell me what you know!" Sam exploded.

He got Mary's attention. She seemed to snap back to reality. "I just wanted David to be happy."

"I don't care about your motives, lady. I want to know where Callie is!"

"I don't know!" Mary retorted. "I only knew about the kidnapping."

Mason cursed.

Sam felt heartsick. When Callie learned of Mary's complicity, it would be quite a blow. Assuming he found her before York killed her.

"How could you do that to Callie?" Walters asked.

"A little late for you to be playing father of the year, don't you think?" Sam said.

Walters lowered his head. "I never wanted any harm to come to her. I just wanted her to understand that it was wrong of her to have slept with her own brother."

"What did you think it did to her when you turned your back on her when she needed you the most?"

"What she did was wrong!" Walters insisted.

"We can debate that from now until hell freezes over later. Right now I want to know where I can find Jim York."

"It wasn't her fault," Mary whispered softly. "David was intrigued by her beauty and her innocence. He never meant for her to get pregnant, he just wanted to…to…"

"Have sex with her," Sam thundered.

Mary was sobbing. "Brittany was so strong and she intimidated my David. He went to Callie because of her sweetness. He never meant her any harm."

"You're pathetic," Sam spat.

"I honestly don't know where she is," Mary said. "I haven't heard from Jim York since the day he called me to tell me Callie had dinner with you."

"Why did he call you?"

"Because I'm the one who has been sending the letters. I thought it would help Callie deal with the fact that the baby was gone. I wanted to help her without hurting my son."

"The threats?" Sam countered.

Mary shook her head. "Not threats. I only ever tried to let Callie know how the baby was doing."

"The update letters. Those were yours?"

Mary nodded. "I couldn't stand seeing her so upset. I thought the letters would bring her comfort."

"How did this plan work?" Seth asked.

Mary let out a slow breath and wiped her eyes with a rumpled tissue. "David said that if Callie had the baby, Brittany wouldn't marry him. I went to Brittany and pleaded with her to change her mind. You see, David truly loves her."

Sam heard the approach of sirens. "Goody for him," he snarled. "So you and David got together with York and planned the kidnapping? David knew Lynn through Brittany and you just handed off your own grandson?"

"Don't say another word," Brittany hissed as she and David and Jim York were brought into the house.

Sam went right for York's throat. If it hadn't been for the two officers and Seth, Sam probably would have killed him right there.

York, who was handcuffed, was tossed into the nearest chair. He glared alternately at Sam and Brittany.

"What is all this?" David asked. "Why is my mother crying?"

"Three guesses," Sam answered.

"I told them the truth," Mary said.

"What truth?" David demanded. Then turning to Brittany, he asked, "Why was Jim York hiding in our basement?"

"Shut up, David," Brittany said. "I called my attorneys. They should be here soon. This is all a misunderstanding. I had no idea Jim was a killer when I told him he could stay with us."

"Hold on!" York yelled. He was pushed down into the chair by the officer guarding him. "I didn't kill anyone, it was her!"

"Brit," David began, "what is he talking about?"

"I don't know," Brittany insisted.

"Like hell you don't," York said. Then to Sam he said, "She paid me to steal the baby. She had me deliver it to her friend Lynn. Lynn was supposed to go back to Ohio with the kid, but she didn't." York laughed. "Lynn pulled a fast one on Brittany and stayed around. She married you. All I did was try to make a profit off that fact. She's your killer! I can prove it—I'll tell you where she had me put Callie. She's out—"

York's last word was swallowed up by the shot from the gun Walters had left by the door.

"Brittany!" David said in horror. "You shot him!"

"Shut up, David," Brittany seethed as she waved the gun around. "Officer, give me your keys."

The patrolman looked to Seth, who nodded. A set of keys to the patrolman's car were tossed to Brittany.

"What are you doing?" David implored, taking a step forward. Brittany leveled the gun on David and pulled the trigger, then ran.

Mary screamed, but Seth and Sam raced out and

tackled Brittany before she could get to the car. She struggled fiercely, then a wicked smile appeared on her face. "Go ahead and arrest me. I choose to remain silent. While I'm silent, little Callie will freeze to death."

Sam's phone rang. He immediately dug it out of his jacket. Brittany was still taunting him with her right to remain silent.

"Hi, Daddy."

He could barely hear Kevin over Brittany. "Hi, pal, listen, now isn't—"

"Why are you with the lunch lady?" Kevin asked.

"What?"

"I hear her voice. I thought you were going to find Callie."

"I will, pal. I've got to keep looking, okay?"

"'Kay."

"Was that the little love child?" Brittany purred as Seth tightened the handcuffs. "Ouch!"

"Gee, did I hurt you?" Seth asked.

True to her word, Brittany remained silent in the hour it took her attorneys to get to the Walters ranch. Mary had been taken by ambulance to the hospital. She collapsed just seconds after David took his final breath. York's body was removed as well.

"I'm Greg Patterson, from Patterson and Getga."

Sam went up to the smarmy attorney and got into his face. "Your client just shot two people in front of all these officers. If she doesn't—"

Seth interrupted. "I'll ask the DA for leniency if she tells us where Callie Walters is right now."

Patterson seemed overwhelmed by all the anger, and he asked to be given some privacy to speak to his client and that her handcuffs be removed, since he might need her to sign some documents. Walters showed him into a back bedroom.

As soon as the door was closed, Sam went down the hallway and put his ear to the door. Brittany was being no more cooperative with her lawyer. Sam wanted to go in and thrash the information out of her. Occasionally he heard laughter, but nothing he could latch on to.

"…they'll have to…hunt for her," Brittany giggled.

Sam raced back up the hall to Mason Walters. "Isn't there a hunting cabin here?"

He nodded.

Then they heard the sound of glass breaking. Patterson came racing out of the room, yelling, "She jumped!"

Sam and Seth both cursed, grabbed their jackets and went outside. It was snowing heavily again. They could barely see two feet in front of them.

Walters came out and led them to where Brittany had broken the window and jumped out. There were a few drops of blood, and Sam trudged through knee-deep snow, trying to follow her trail.

"She must have gone to the stable!" Walters yelled. "Head a little more east!"

The three men arrived at the stable only to find Brittany had taken a horse and left. "We can try to follow her tracks," Walters suggested.

Taking a chance, Sam yelled, "No, let's go straight to the hunting cabin."

CALLIE HEARD SOMETHING over the sound of the strong wind. The snow had drifted above the window, so she had no way to tell if someone was coming to her rescue, or coming to kill her. Callie stood poised, her weapon hidden in her paper-covered hands.

She heard the sound of the lock click, and then the wind blew the door opened.

"Brittany?" She was genuinely shocked. She'd expected her father, not Brittany and a shotgun.

"Glad we're having this opportunity for a face-to-face."

"You were behind this? Not Daddy?"

Callie saw a flicker of black in the blinding snow. She prayed it was Sam. Mindful that Brittany would have a clear shot of anyone approaching, Callie moved around the room so that there was no way she could see out the open door.

"Stay still."

"Why? You shot Mrs. Lange in a moving car."

"I am a four-time junior target champion. If I wanted to, I could probably part your hair with this thing."

"What did I ever do to you?"

"You got pregnant," Brittany said.

"So what? I was happy to raise my baby alone."

"I don't want children. I don't like them."

"Brittany?" Callie tried to reason. "David signed

his parental rights away yesterday. Sam is Kevin's father. We don't want David in our lives.''

"David thinks differently. I told him I didn't want children. When you found the little brat and Mary told him, David was all set to claim his son. I couldn't have that. After Jim York hit you, I took your files, hoping to wipe away any traces of the little brat. Lynn double-crossed me. She said she'd take the baby back to Ohio. Instead she married Landry and stayed. I even had to see the brat from time to time. Thanks to Lynn, I've been paying York blackmail for years. I hate you all.''

"You didn't have to. I don't want David in my life.''

"He wouldn't have been, once the baby was gone. Everything would have worked out, if only Lynn hadn't tried to screw York over.''

Callie saw three distinct outlines coming toward the cabin. "How did she do that?''

"Lynn refused to keep paying her finder's fee.''

"Finder's fee?''

Brittany rolled her eyes impatiently. "Once Lynn married into the Landry family, York blackmailed her, too. Then one day she decided to stop paying. She was going to tell her husband the truth. Or some version of it, anyway.''

"So York rigged the accident?''

"No, I did. A very nice job, if I do say so myself. No one even considered it wasn't an accident.''

"Wasn't Lynn your friend?''

Brittany shrugged. "She worked one semester in

my sorority house in Ohio. She told me her sad tale of an early hysterectomy, so when I heard you were pregnant, I called Lynn in Ohio, and she couldn't get out here fast enough.''

"How did you hook up with York?" Callie asked. She easily made out Sam's shape among the trio. She had to keep him safe.

"Met him here," Brittany taunted. "Gosh, little mother-in-law Mary introduced us. As you know, he would do anything for a dollar."

"Would? Past tense?"

"He died earlier."

Callie felt a tickle of fear. "Of what?"

"An open mouth," Brittany answered. "You are my last loose end. Or I might kill the kid before I go. I haven't decided."

"Go where?" Callie asked as Sam reached the doorway.

"I have a private jet. I'll take a long vacation somewhere without an extradition treaty with the U.S. Now that I'm a widow, I'm free to go anywhere."

"You killed David?"

Brittany shrugged. "He was the perfect husband, except when it came to all this baby crap. We were fighting about that the other day when you stopped by the dealership. I knew then that you'd never leave us alone. I knew I couldn't stay married to a man pining after some little bastard child."

A large clump of snow fell from Sam's hat, gaining Brittany's attention when he was still too far away to protect himself from the gun.

Without thinking, Callie jumped forward and grabbed the muzzle of the rifle. At the same time she stabbed Brittany with the earpiece from the sunglasses she had discovered earlier.

Then everything was a blur. She saw Seth come in and get Brittany around the throat. A shot went off, and she felt herself being pulled out into the snow. She looked up into Sam's eyes.

"Are you okay?" Sam asked, touching her face.

"Just cold," she said. "I missed you."

"Is she all right?"

At the gruff voice, Callie looked past Sam and saw her father. She felt guilty for thinking him capable of masterminding all this chaos. "I'm fine," she said.

"Put this around you," her father said, offering her a blanket. "Climb on up here, and I'll give you a ride home."

Callie started to cry. "Thanks, Daddy." Sam helped her to her feet, then up onto the back of the horse. "Have you stopped hating me?"

"I never did hate you. And I'm sorry. I'll explain it all on the ride back."

Seth subdued Brittany and put her back in handcuffs.

Sam could barely contain himself as Seth marched her by. God forgive him, but he wanted to kill her for all the evil things she had done, not just to his family, but to hers.

CALLIE WAS BACK in a hospital gown and was not too thrilled by the situation, Sam concluded as he went into the cubicle of the emergency room.

"Getting all put together?"

She smiled. "Yes. I've got three new stitches at the back of my head, but no other injuries or trauma."

"Good," Sam said, staring at the floor as he silently practiced his speech. "Callie?"

"Sam?"

They smiled at each other. "You go first," he told Callie.

"You go first," she countered.

"No, you."

"No, you."

"This is getting a little silly," Sam admitted. "I'll go. I've spent the last two hours in the waiting room practicing for this moment."

"Did my father leave?"

"He's with Mary. They admitted her—she had a heart attack."

Callie squeezed her eyes shut for a moment. "Never in a million years would I have guessed Mary was part of the scheme."

"A small part," Sam reminded her. "I think David dying in her lap is probably punishment enough. She only did the things she did to ensure David had a happy life."

"I guess."

"Wouldn't you walk through fire for Kevin? Well, I suppose that's how Mary got caught up in all this."

She met his eyes. "I'd walk through fire for you, too."

Sam felt his heart swell. "Is that your way of telling me you love me?"

"Pretty much," she admitted.

Sam gently kissed her. It lasted a long time. Until Chance returned.

"We've got people working here," Chance teased.

"I'm working," Sam said. "I'm working on asking her to marry me."

"That's good because—"

"Chance likes me," Callie interrupted. "Right, Chance?"

He shrugged and winked. "Give me a call in the morning. I'll have those test results for you then."

Sam was concerned. "What tests? I thought you said everything was fine."

"It is," Chance assured him. "I suggest you take her home and put her to bed. *Alone.*"

"WHAT ARE YOU DOING OUT of bed?" Sam admonished.

"I've been lying around for almost a week. You've been pretty scarce," Callie said.

"I've been getting caught up at work, and I was just being patient. You told me not to press you."

Callie came over and sat in his lap. "So press me, already."

Sam could hear Kevin's footfalls on the steps. "This will have to be quick.… Will you marry me?"

Callie nodded and kissed him. Until she felt Kevin

tug on the hem of her robe. "Morning," she said to him. Kevin was still a tad shy. "I've been keeping a secret, want me to whisper it to you?"

Kevin nodded.

Callie whispered something in his ear that made him frown. Sam frowned, too. "What's a' matter, pal? You'll get to be the ring bearer or something."

"'Kay." He put his hand on Callie's abdomen and asked, "Are you sure there's a baby in there?"

Callie met Sam's astonished but happy eyes and nodded. "I do love you."

"How did this happen?" Sam asked.

"Uncle Chance can 'splain it," Kevin offered. "He told me all about it!"

They're strong, sexy, protective,
and they're coming your way soon…

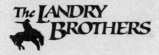
The **LANDRY BROTHERS**

*Turn the page for a peek at what's in
store for you in Kelsey Roberts's next*

LANDRY BROTHERS *book,
coming to you in January 2000.*

#545 LANDRY'S LAW

Only from Harlequin Intrigue!

Prologue

Snow crunched beneath his boots as Sheriff Seth Landry cautiously made his way down the steep bank to the crime scene. Flurries still swirled in the air as he greeted his deputy, J. D. Lindsay.

"Has the coroner been called?"

J.D. nodded, then blew warm breath into his cupped hands. "As far as I know, no one has touched a thing."

"Who called it in?" Seth asked.

J.D. pointed toward the Mountainview Inn behind them. "One of the guests. Ken Updyke. He's passing through on his way to Seattle. He was out jogging and came upon this."

Seth regarded the scene. The snowstorm had pretty much obliterated the area around the body. He stepped forward and knelt to get a better look at the victim. Judging from the small entrance wound at the back of the guy's head, Seth figured the weapon was a .22.

Seth also noted that the man's clothing wasn't right. He was wearing a suit beneath a camouflage down jacket but didn't have any gloves on. Seth made a mental note of that inconsistency.

"Looks just like the last one," J.D. remarked.

Seth's gut knotted at the mere suggestion. Jasper, Montana, was a small, out-of-the-way town where everyone knew everyone else. Tourists passed through to visit some of the quaint shops and historic markers in the area. To date, none of them had turned out to be serial killers. If he actually had a serial killer on his hands.

"Anyone know who he is?" Seth asked the half dozen or so onlookers who had gathered. The victim was on his stomach, but his face was turned to one side.

"Isn't that Harvey Whitlock?" one of them asked.

Seth adjusted his position and tilted his head to get a better look. "It appears so."

"He's only lived here a couple of months," J.D. said. "I guess that's long enough to make an enemy."

Seth stood as the coroner arrived. He shook hands with Dr. Hall. "Sorry to get you out so early," Seth said when he watched the doctor shifting from one foot to the other in an apparent attempt to ward off the cold.

"I'm getting too old for this," Hall grumbled. "Isn't that Harvey Whitlock?"

Seth nodded. Dr. Hall handed J.D. a camera and instructed him on where and when to take photographs of the victim.

The idea that there might be some deranged killer running loose in his town still distracted Seth. He pulled out his notepad and started making some notations.

By the time Dr. Hall was ready to have the officers turn the body over, the ambulance crew and at least a dozen more gawkers had arrived. Seth silently hoped his own death would be more private. Not some public spectacle like poor Harvey's.

J.D. took the victim's feet, the ambulance guys the midsection, and Seth took the head. With practiced precision, they turned Harvey over so that he could be placed on a stretcher, then whisked away from the prying, morbid eyes of the crowd.

"What's that?" Seth asked, pointing to Harvey's left palm.

They all moved in for a closer look. The frigid water from the creek had washed away the writing until it was very faint.

"Savannah, nine, one, two," Seth read aloud.

"Looks like part of a phone number," J.D. said excitedly.

Seth was puzzled. If he recalled correctly, Harvey was from someplace in the Midwest, not the South. He breathed a little easier. There had been no writing on the hand of the first victim. Maybe the two cases weren't related.

"I don't think that's a phone number," came a voice from the crowd.

Seth turned and looked in the direction of the voice. It was a man in his early thirties. He had the dress and manner of a yuppie tourist. Seth went over to the man.

"Why not?"

The yuppie shrugged. "I saw him last night in the bar."

"And?" Seth prompted.

"He was staring at the clock."

"When was this?" Seth asked.

"Maybe ten after nine or so."

"And you're sure it was him?"

The yuppie insisted that it was.

"How can you be sure? You aren't a local."

"I remember him because of the babe who showed up to meet him. I mean, no offense to the dead or anything, but that guy isn't exactly *GQ* material, and he manages to snag the prettiest woman in the place."

"What did she look like?"

"Pretty, brown hair, incredible green eyes, a body to die for—sorry, I didn't mean—I mean—"

"Did you happen to hear him call her by name?"

The yuppie nodded with enthusiasm. "That's why I don't think that the writing on his hand is a phone number."

"Because?" Seth prodded.

"Because he called the woman Savannah."

Seth swallowed, hard. *Savannah Wyatt.*

Don't miss Seth's story

#545 LANDRY'S LAW

coming to you in January 2000.

Only from Kelsey Roberts and Harlequin Intrigue!

If you enjoyed what you just read,
then we've got an offer you can't resist!

Take 2 bestselling love stories FREE!
Plus get a FREE surprise gift!

Clip this page and mail it to Harlequin Reader Service®

IN U.S.A.
3010 Walden Ave.
P.O. Box 1867
Buffalo, N.Y. 14240-1867

IN CANADA
P.O. Box 609
Fort Erie, Ontario
L2A 5X3

YES! Please send me 2 free Harlequin Intrigue® novels and my free surprise gift. Then send me 4 brand-new novels every month, which I will receive months before they're available in stores. In the U.S.A., bill me at the bargain price of $3.34 plus 25¢ delivery per book and applicable sales tax, if any*. In Canada, bill me at the bargain price of $3.71 plus 25¢ delivery per book and applicable taxes**. That's the complete price and a savings of over 10% off the cover prices—what a great deal! I understand that accepting the 2 free books and gift places me under no obligation ever to buy any books. I can always return a shipment and cancel at any time. Even if I never buy another book from Harlequin, the 2 free books and gift are mine to keep forever. So why not take us up on our invitation. You'll be glad you did!

181 HEN CNEZ
381 HEN CNE3

Name	(PLEASE PRINT)
Address	Apt.#
City	State/Prov.	Zip/Postal Code

* Terms and prices subject to change without notice. Sales tax applicable in N.Y.
** Canadian residents will be charged applicable provincial taxes and GST.
  All orders subject to approval. Offer limited to one per household.
  ® are registered trademarks of Harlequin Enterprises Limited.

INT99

"This book is DYNAMITE!"
—Kristine Rolofson

"A riveting page turner…"
—Joan Elliott Pickart

"Enough twists and turns to keep everyone guessing… What a ride!"
—Jule McBride

See what all your favorite authors are talking about.

Coming October 1999 to a retail store near you.

HARLEQUIN®
Makes any time special ™

WIN A DREAM

In celebration of Harlequin®'s golden anniversary

Enter to win a *dream!* You could win:

- A luxurious trip for two to *The Renaissance Cottonwoods Resort* in Scottsdale, Arizona, or

- A bouquet of flowers once a week for a year from **FTD**, or

- A $500 shopping spree, or

- A fabulous bath & body gift basket, including **K-tel**'s *Candlelight and Romance* 5-CD set.

Look for **WIN A DREAM** flash on specially marked Harlequin® titles by Penny Jordan, Dallas Schulze, Anne Stuart and Kristine Rolofson in October 1999*.

FTD

RENAISSANCE.
COTTONWOODS RESORT
SCOTTSDALE, ARIZONA

K·TEL

COMING NEXT MONTH

#537 MEMORIES AT MIDNIGHT by Joanna Wayne
The McCord Family Countdown

Darlene Remington couldn't remember who wanted her dead, but she recognized Sheriff Clint Richards easily—she'd walked away from his strong, protective arms six years ago. Seeing Darlene again reminded Clint just how much he needed a woman in his life— Darlene, to be specific. In a race to find her would-be killer, was Clint ready to confront his past...and willing to risk his heart?

#538 NO BABY BUT MINE by Carly Bishop

Thrown together by tragedy, Kirsten McCourt and Garrett Weisz had shared one night of compassion—and pleasure. Five years later, caught in the grasp of a powerful vigilante leader, Kirsten and Garrett are reunited by danger. Determined to keep Kirsten safe and in his life, Garrett will stop at nothing to obtain justice—especially when he finds that her kidnapped son is also his....

#539 FOR HIS DAUGHTER by Dani Sinclair

Accused of his ex-wife's murder, with no memory of the night in question, Officer Lee Garvey turned to Kayla Coughlin for help. Kayla had never trusted the police, but Lee's obvious devotion to his two-year-old daughter made it difficult to believe the man could be capable of murder—and their mutual attraction made him hard to resist....

#540 WHEN NIGHT DRAWS NEAR by Lisa Bingham

When their plane makes an emergency landing in the snowy wilderness of the Rocky Mountains, Elizabeth Boothe and Seth Brody must fight against an unknown killer and the still-smoldering attraction of their failed marriage. Stranded, with only each other to trust, the couple must overcome both danger and desire to make it off the mountain alive....